The Killers Above

MAX HAMMER

The Killers Above

A Novel

New York

For all those who revere the sacred

and fight to protect it...

Acknowledgements

My sincere thanks to Lorraine, who proved to be an invaluable editor, and to all those who made this work possible.

Especially, I give thanks to the spirit of all those Native Americans that I have known or read, of many tribes and nations, and others who have helped me, through their lives, their words, and their work, to see and to understand the worlds beyond the world we know.

...And when the last Red Man shall have perished, and the memory of my tribe shall have become a myth among the White Men, these shores will swarm with the invisible dead of my tribe, and when your children's children think themselves alone in the field, the store, the shop, upon the highway, or in the silence of the pathless woods, they will not be alone. In all the Earth there is no place dedicated to solitude. At night when the streets of your cities and villages are silent and you think them deserted, they will throng with the returning hosts that once filled them and still love this beautiful land.

The White Man will never be alone.

Let him be just and deal kindly with my people, for the dead are not powerless.

Dead, did I say? There is no death, only a change of worlds.

– Chief Seattle of the Duwamish,
1854, Puget Sound

The Elders
on the Shore

The Puget Sound is not the sea. On the shore, there is only a quiet lapping. The roaming pulse of the tide breathes through a hundred inlets, marking each moment upon the land. Rising dawn mists like clouds birth momentary landscapes, where at end of day spires of spruce and fir float in the last dusky tremors of dusk. Overhead, the distant calls of geese break a silence so deep it drums the ears.

The mists are always moving. Everywhere, the marsh grass is silent witness to the tides, to the ebb and flow of seasons, to the dawn and dusk of centuries.

History, time, was for the White man. Frank Johnson knew that, as he slowly walked the water's edge, the soft wet mud sucking at the soles of his shoes. Leading the horse on which his mother rode, he carefully threaded his way around the outbursts of tiny crabs scurrying at his feet.

He was old, very old, his face long since become leathery folds encasing the deep wells of long-saddened eyes, but she *was older, ancient, hardly of this world. In her eyes still moved the dark shadows of the countless seasons she had endured, her ancestors had endured. These were the shadows of a violent world, the violent coming of the white settlers, the building of the city of Seattle across the bay... And for all of it, her people had paid a terrible price.*

But now even the voices of her grandchildren, and their children, had long since faded in her ears. Time. What was real? Steel and concrete and ships and smokestacks? Or the laughter of children as they fished in the salmon streams, the chattering of her grandmothers as they wove their cedar baskets?

In her mind, one memory followed the next until all returned to the beginning, to her own childhood in a free land....and ever and ever the memories flowed...time...was a circle. She lived at its center. Now this mile of coastline was all that remained, for her and her son.

Every day, they traveled it. For many decades now, was it seven, or eight, or even nine, they had breathed the wind of this shore. As another piece was taken from them, and another, and another, they had deepened their communion with this remaining mile. Here, their lives lived, at this meeting of worlds. This small bit of earth was their Earth, and the Earth of their vanished tribe. No power in heaven or on earth would deny them this inheritance they loved.

In the great circle of time, they would be walking this shore forever.

David Ames looked through the side window of his polished white limousine at the muddy shoreline, more than a mile of coastline owned by his corporation, held by law in temporary trust. It was a boon granted by his Board of Directors, responding to the recommendation of a public relations firm to quiet, for a time, the public outcry over that ownership.

Now the years had passed, and all was forgotten. The plan had worked.

It only remained for him to complete the unpleasant task of removing these two last Indians, native Americans–he knew the proper words...

His limousine raced along the dirt road hugging the curving shoreline of the Puget Sound. He was nervous. It had been his concern and appeals to the Board that had extended to these last two inhabitants these years of grace. It seemed the only decent thing to do. Now, finally, the Board had demanded the land, and it had fallen upon him, as president, to inform them. So, he steeled himself to the task.

The limousine stopped. David could see the two of them on the shore, one riding a horse, the other walking and leading the horse, through his window. The door was opened for him, and he stepped out into the brisk autumn air, onto the wet hard mud beneath his feet. He hailed them with an uncertain wave of his hand, but they did not stop.

He summoned a stern determination to brush away his own lack of resolve and began walking briskly across the beach. The mud splattered the trousers of his thousand-dollar-suit, and somewhere, in that fifty-yard walk, without knowing, he crossed an invisible boundary. He crossed from his world into theirs, from his time into their time. It was a time that he would never understand, a time incomprehensible to any White man.

He moved now within a dream, still believing he was the executive, and them...and them, the tenants on this company land...not knowing he was only an actor in a play whose author would forever remain hidden to him. He caught up to them and offered his hand to the old man walking, who turned and stared at him, and stopped the horse. David looked up to the old woman, who remained sitting on her horse with her back to him.

Now he was telling them. The words were coming out of his mouth, his genuine sorrow, his real compassion. They must obey, as he must obey, what had been decreed by a power higher than himself–the Board had voted. There were laws within corporations, bylaws, and regulations.

But from his mouth there was no sound. No one heard his words, even himself. Like the roar of an ancient river, a greater silence descended upon them, possessing all minds and voices, so that his voice become the mouthpiece between worlds, of one world speaking to another. And for eyes that could see, and hearts that could feel, forces were invoked, furies unleashed, and an unseen shadow descended upon that place where he was now standing.

The old woman saw it. Until this time unmoving, she now turned slowly to let her gaze fall upon him. It was a vast ancient gaze, like an ancient burning wind, burning and branding upon him the wrathful condemnation for every rape and killing, every violent and violating act, and now, for this, this one final act of horrible, unforgivable transgression.

He froze, locked within her stare, existing nowhere but through her eyes. He was the captive, made to bear all the hatred of a murdered race...until at last the light in those eyes softened, became the wisdom of an old woman, the kindness of a grandmother with a great and wise soul. She was looking upon him now with infinite compassion, because now that was all that could be.

He was confused. A chill ran down his spine. He did not know that she was seeing the terror that would befall him for the sins of those that had come before. He only knew, suddenly, he had to make it back to his limousine.

He lowered his gaze, and as a man fleeing a wild animal, hastened back to the safety of his car and driver.

A Man Chasing Images

At three A.M., few lights were burning in the warehouse district of Seattle. On the sixth floor of one converted industrial building, a few rays of light escaped the huge, black-shaded windows of Johnny Hammond's photographic studio. Through the iron-framed windows, a shadow moved across the fine vertical lines of light, one after the other, from left to right, and back again.

Johnny Hammond, photographer, part-time private investigator, part-time security jock, was pacing the floor. He knew he was pacing. It made him pace even more. He was 38 years old, 6'2", almost ten years out from the Green Berets, from the ghosts of the Phoenix project, still with the lean and muscular physique that had never left him.

On the wall, three large portraits of one woman rushed by him as he walked. It was his work. His work of her, a perfect photographic image of her, Lara—Lara who had vanished, vanished into the arms of another man.

He had met her at the Pike Place Market on a sunny Saturday morning. Now he counted off the years...seven years with her, three more lost without her, and after that, more years under the shadows of their time together. He had lost himself in his work, in other women.

Until now. The years had passed. He had tried to forget her. Time had passed, too much time. What did he have to show for it? Yet the shadow of that lost love had left its mark on all he had tried since then, leaving only lost beginnings and self-imposed isolation. He looked around at his bare surroundings. Hardly any comfort at all. Better just to serve his own art, his new mistress, no matter how fierce and jealous, or unpredictable, to glimpse for the briefest moment again that inspiration he had first found in the one who now he held as only the faintest memory.

So, he had returned to the image of Lara, where his journey had begun, not to mourn a lost relationship, but just hoping it might help him find his way home. So, he had found another to photograph.

The hours were passing. Seven AM.

There was a knock on the door. Chemical delivery.

He rushed to the door but barely opened it, snaking his hand through to return with a bottle of photo developing fluid. He stared at the label, this power he now held in his hand, this key to another kingdom...just forward, he told himself, just forward and keep moving.

He walked to his darkroom door across the room. Once inside, he clicked on the red light. Now there was a rhythm to his movements, moving him deep into the enchanted world of the image, the spirit he made visible to human eyes...

Here is where he let that distant world of war fade and grow distant, its cutting shadows to no longer burning him, but retreating in the light of her image, like cool water...his hands worked the chemical bath, the paper, the tongs, in a gentle mechanical dance...and in the dim light she began to appear, this woman of mesmerizing eyes...full lips...high sculptured cheek-bones...she was seventeen when he had found her and she had never been photographed.

"Come on, come on..." he intoned, as though coaxing Aphrodite herself into mortal form.

She had come for one afternoon for a photo session. He could not remember her last name, maybe had never asked. He had photographed her with the Hasselblad large format camera he had inherited from his father and had never seen her again. Just images, images becoming images, revolving one around the other.

Delicately lifting the photographic, he moved it into the adjacent chemical bath, and laid down the tongs. The doorbell rang, breaking his concentration. Hastily, without looking, he grabbed the tongs from the wrong tray and removed the photograph. He realized at once he had marked it.

"Damn it!" He hit the button of the door buzzer, and heard the front door opening, and footsteps approaching. He picked up the photo again, glancing at the marred finish.

"Johnny?" the voice asked through the darkroom door.

He recognized the voice of David Ames.

"Hang on, David," Johnny answered.

With one last look at the marred photograph, he tossed it down into a waste pile, along with the tongs.

"Come on in."

David entered the dark room, light flooding through the open door.

"Someone in here with you?" David half-joked.

"Never alone," Johnny answered, speaking in a shorthand he and David spoke from years of conversations.

David was handsome, with steel blue eyes in a full head of combed black hair, with that perfect executive physique you see in magazine advertisements for men's suits. Johnny smiled to himself. David was one friend in whom he had confided some of the passions of his search, although not all.

"Wicked dreams...won't take you where you need to go..." David answered.

"Just looking for a way home..." Johnny and David spoke in unison, in easy camaraderie.

"So, how ya' doin', David?"

"Fine," David answered. "Yeah..."

Johnny gave him a sideways glance. "So that's why you're here? You're fine?" Johnny always knew when there was something bothering David, and for some reason tonight he was feeling unusually blunt.

"Yeah..." David confessed. "I need to talk to you."

"Come on." Johnny led him back into the living room and opened the three huge window shades. The full moon flooded the room with light, showing the white silver of the snow-capped Olympic range across the dark waters of the Puget Sound.

David turned to revel in the view. Johnny was happy he had it to offer.

He had worked hard to build his studio, years of commercial jobs that had rubbed against his grain.

David noticed the skyscraper opposite. "New building," he commented.

"They're on strike," Johnny said. "Here." Johnny handed him a bottle of beer.

"No, no thanks, Johnny," David answered.

David lifted his gaze again to the horizon and stood staring across the expanse.

Johnny just shook his head, moving behind his Hasselblad mounted on a tripod. David had come to him many times in the course of their friendship. He was glad David confided in him and valued his opinion. In the viewfinder, Johnny framed David against the panoramic skyline, glass skyscrapers, and the Olympic mountains across the Puget Sound. He took the shot.

David turned with the sound of the shutter but said nothing.

Johnny watched David's mood turn from reverie into distress.

Finally, David said, "I can't stall the Board any longer. I got to move them, Johnny."

"Native Americans have lived on that piece of land for more than a thousand years, David."

"I spoke to them today..." David said.

Johnny waited for more.

"Her eyes...that old woman..." David intoned, haunted.

"She's guarding the ghosts of her ancestors, David. What did you expect?"

David was a good man, Johnny thought, but he was trying to understand something he really had no hope of ever understanding.

Off to his left, David watched an unharnessed steel worker deftly walk the exposed steel beam of a newly rising skyscraper, entranced with his high-wire ballet. Wrapped in his own thoughts and strangely nervous, he turned toward Johnny for some support.

"Johnny, I wanted to talk to you about—" David caught himself, for the first time noticing the torn portrait of Lara on the floor. With sincere caring, he asked, "You two ever going to see each other again?"

Johnny shook his head. He could not begin to tell anyone, not even David. He and David had grown close, these past years, as their professional association had warmed into a genuine friendship, but this pain he bore too deep. He could not share it with anyone.

A moment of uneasy silence grew between them, as Johnny waited for David to tell him the real purpose of his visit.

David finally spoke. "I'm nervous about the reception on the plaza tomorrow, Johnny. Another death threat came in last night. And our Japanese financiers will be there."

"By phone?" Johnny asked.

"Letter, same as before," David answered.

"Any reason to take it more seriously than before?" Johnny asked.

David seemed almost embarrassed, but also relieved. "No, I guess not."

"I'll be there. Nothing's going to happen," Johnny said.

They stood looking at one another.

"I knew I could count on you. I'm grateful, really...you've got your new business now and ..."

Johnny, reading the fear and concern in David's face, nodded reassuringly, his expression growing more businesslike.

"It's alright, David." Johnny said. "I'll be there."

Send the bill directly to my office?" David asked.

Johnny shook his head, clasping David's arms.

"Bill? Come on! Dinner at Canlis. You bring the ladies," Johnny said easily.

David, still nervous, tried to smile. "You got it."

Johnny showed him toward the door. "Now why don't you go home and get some rest. I need to get back to work."

David turned back appreciatively. "Johnny, if anything happens to me, look out for my brothers."

Johnny watched David disappear through the door. For the briefest moment, something passed over him, something without color or shape, only an emptiness reaching into him. The feeling passed and he thought nothing more of it.

He only felt how tired he was, and how much he did not want to go back to that world. It was a world of harsh angles and calculating motives, built upon centuries of lies. Security work was only something he had been forced to pursue to make ends meet. But a promise was a promise, and a friend, a friend.

The Killers Above

The next morning, on the plaza of the Chilkat Corporation skyscraper, a lively well-dressed crowd including reporters and camera crews awaited the arrival of coming dignitaries.

The new glass tower building shot forty-eight stories into the sky. On the upper floors, the strong wind rippled the reflections of clouds in the huge wall-sized panes of gleaming sunlit glass.

At his studio, Johnny was still sleeping uneasily in the chair. He awoke with a start. The sun was pouring in through the windows. What time was it? Goddammit, what time was it?! He grabbed for his clock—11:02—the alarm had not gone off! He had set it! He could not have slept through it! He tossed it down.

"Damn it!"

He swung out of the chair to his desk, anxiously opening his top desk drawer, frantically searching, finally yanking the drawer out to dump its contents onto a table, grabbing the black service pistol that clattered out.

Back at the Chilkat Tower Plaza, an elegant white stretch limousine was slowly approaching the skyscraper.

From inside, in a top-floor boardroom with a panoramic view of the city and Puget Sound, two blue-suited executives watched it on the street far below.

Inside the limousine, David and his brother William spoke to a Japanese businessman, Mr. Itomi, sitting across.

"Mr. Itomi, Americans have the shortest memories in the world," William Ames offered. "The public outcry will be forgotten in a month. Then only two nearly dead Indians will still be complaining about this deal."

David shifted uneasily in his seat but said nothing. He knew the deal was too important to let his personal feelings interfere.

Mr. Itomi simply nodded, acknowledging his comments without revealing his opinion.

William forced an uneasy smile, uncertain of Mr. Itomi's response, hoping for the best.

Not far away, Johnny raced his sedan through the city streets, swerving wildly and dangerously through traffic. Wheeling around a corner, he ran into stopped traffic– several cars and a stopped flatbed truck, its load of barrels dumped on the road. He slammed the steering wheel.

"Nooo!!!"

He jammed on his breaks, throwing the car into reverse, but traffic behind him boxed him in.

"Come on!"

He threw the car into forward—it lurched up on the curb. He flung open the door and took off running, his training kicking in as he took in the scene he was passing.

Behind the overturned truck was a black limousine. Standing next to it were two men, a Japanese businessman trying to impress urgency to his driver. In the limousine's open window, he saw a beautiful young Japanese woman in a ceremonial blue silk kimono, peering out.

Johnny ran up to the truck, opened the cab door. The driver was gone—he glanced around. This was wrong, very wrong. He controlled his near panic, and began running, his senses wired. Sweat began running down his face, his breath heaving. He turned a corner and saw the plaza of the Chilkat Corporation tower a half-block ahead.

The limousine carrying David, William, and Mr. Itomi was arriving.

The crowd was moving forward, pressing against the security guards maintaining the reserved inner circle.

Hundreds of demonstrators waved signs and shouted: "Return Native American Lands Now!" and "Stop the Exploitation!" and "End Corporate Rule!"

David, William, and Mr. Itomi emerged from the limousine, trying to ignore the demonstrators. David smiled to Mr. Itomi, and grandly waved upward, showing off his skyscraper like a proud father.

Mr. Itomi looked up and nodded respectfully, suitably impressed.

David threw a nervous glance over his shoulder hoping to see Johnny.

Johnny reached the outer edge of the crowd and began frantically weaving his way toward the center.

The crowd surged toward the three executives as they walked across the plaza toward the main entrance, the security agents closing ranks to withstand the onrush.

David and William were sharing greetings and shaking hands with the various dignitaries.

Ten feet away from them, Johnny stopped, and with cool penetrating precision, began scanning the demonstrators, every face, every pair of eyes, hands, as they approached. Time began to slow as his mind and senses approached fever pitch. There was something—he knew there was something.

There was somebody here—where were they? Who was it? But he saw no one, only businessman, attorneys, spectators, nothing suspicious, and with every passing moment grew more anxious.

David, William, and Mr. Itomi came together at a yellow ceremonial ribbon stretched before the tower entrance. Mr. Itomi was handed a large pair of scissors. He waved and smiled to the applauding crowd, and cut the ribbon, handing the scissors back.

William whispered something in Mr. Itomi's ear, and they both took a couple of steps back from David.

Now Johnny's eyes were desperately darting, scanning the demonstrators, as he pushed through the crowd toward David...suddenly, his gaze fixed on a woman, already within the inner circle of dignitaries, wearing a ceremonial blue silk kimono, her eyes locked, hypnotic, as she approached. His eyes scanned every inch of her body, her dress, her ornaments, her make-up, and then he saw it—a half-inch black wire running from her sleeve into a closed fist. He shouted.

"David!!!" Johnny yelled.

The world began to unfold as though in slow motion. David looked over his shoulder toward the familiar voice, as the woman began to bow respectfully before him.

Johnny burst through the crowd, pushing people aside, whipping out his pistol.

"NO!!!!" he shouted.

He fired—his bullet ripped into her chest and the crowd broke into shouts and screams, many throwing themselves upon the ground—the woman staggered back, but inhumanly, as though hypnotized, recovered, trying to continue her bowing motion.

David, frozen in place, looked left and right, as William and Mr. Itomi scattered with the crowd and Johnny fired again—the woman again staggered from the bullet's impact—again she tried to complete her bow.

He fired into her forehead—her head snapped back, lifting and hurtling her body five feet backwards, dead.

The sounds of shouting and running were all around him. David and Johnny looked to one another. David's expression was otherworldly, terrified—he reached out with his eyes to Johnny.

Johnny turned his head in every direction, stalking some unseen threat. An eerie sound came, a descending whistling rush of air.

From where? Johnny shot a glance toward David.

David, still in shock, looked up. A falling twisting mirror of light rushed toward him from above—his eyes opened wide in horror just before the glass crashed down through him, diagonally severing his body from shoulder to hip in a fierce explosion, shooting a red fountain of safety glass fragments thirty feet into the air.

Two sprays of blood, like giant brushstrokes across the morning air's canvas, flew left and right, on one side covering the faces of Johnny and two security guards, and on the other side, the faces of the onlookers.

And then for a brief moment, silence rushed in, and all floated on a motionless sea in the unknown foreboding landscape of another world. Then that doorway into another world closed, and time returned, while the onlookers remained frozen, stunned, but the screams began.

Where David had been standing, only blood remained. Some of the onlookers were looking down to the left, others down to the right, at his severed remains.

For a moment, Johnny, with the rest, stood fixated on the horror, until the horror rose up from his belly and through his throat, until he shouted and raged, "Bastards! Bastards!" his voice reverberating across the plaza.

And then the spell was broken. The first guard knocked the gun out of his hand, while the second threw a chokehold on him from behind. He struggled fiercely to break the guard's grip.

The second guard looked up. "Seal the building!"

Security guards now appeared from every direction, swarming over the plaza, taking control of the panicked crowd. Cries and shouts filled the air. And at that moment he saw her.

At that moment, for the first time in his life, he saw the entrance to a world he knew existed, but never believed he would reach.

As she emerged from the crowd, tall and stately, perfectly dressed and composed in a long white dress, young but not young, he could not take his eyes off her face, as he lost himself in the enthralling vortex of her sensual grace. She moved like a queen, like a cat prowling, stalking the prey of life with an abandon at once fierce and effortless, so that none in heaven or earth could deny her, their questions and doubts melting like markings in the sand under a rising tide.

Nor could he deny her. She moved like lightning into his soul, asking nothing, taking everything, before a word of protest could escape his lips.

Mesmerized by her stunning beauty, he ceased to struggle, watching her, as all watched her, glide across the plaza to look calmly down at the mutilated corpse...so calmly that a peace descended upon the whole crowd, an unnatural, strange, otherworldly peace. He had seen this peace before, in war. It was the peace of all those who fear, not daring to raise their eyes to look upon the face of their gods lest a similar fate be visited upon them.

But she was from another world beyond the reach of both men and gods. Not a single person watching did not feel that privilege in her, although none could imagine how she had come into it. They just kept their distance, witnessing something they would never understand, cringing before a power they would always fear.

To Johnny, she seemed fragile, as vulnerable in each moment as most lives experience in only a handful of moments...so fragile she could not walk the earth—did she walk? —but for the protection of some higher power. But what price had she paid for that certain grace?

She looked up as though feeling his gaze, even his very question, and met his eyes with a penetrating erotic stare that both fascinated and chilled him. Her eyes were a shining sapphire blue and her complexion a fine white porcelain, and in that moment, she took him into another world.

He knew it was her world, a world she ruled only because she suffered its possession of her.

The first guard was moving toward the dead woman.

Again, he violently tried to break free, shouting, "NOOO!"

The guard only tighten his chokehold, but Johnny loosened his hold enough to yell, "She's wired!"

Three more security guards rushed from the building. The first guard was now kneeling beside the fallen women, pulling out a pocketknife, motioning the other guard to move the crowd farther back.

"Get them back! Now! And get that psycho out of here!" the first guard shouted.

The second guard began to drag Johnny off as the first guard cut two seams into the woman's dress, and gently, expertly, pulled back the fabric to reveal the flat layered packs of gray plastic explosives - he shouted to the arriving guards.

"Clear the plaza! It's a bomb!"

Johnny took everything in, the guards, the crowd, the news cameras, but his gaze was returning to her, even as they were dragging him away.

She was looking down again, at the mutilated corpse, but he knew she was holding him in her mind, and in perfectly matching time she lifted her eyes from David's body and returned her gaze to him. It was a strange solemn gaze that reached with cool fingers into his heart, as they dragged him away...

He remembered little of the ride. He had been thrown in the back of a police car, manhandled, cursed and punched. All their questions were just the chattering of gulls on the seashore. He had said nothing, could say nothing.

Now he sat on the floor of his jail cell, his back to the wall, his face in his hands. He was lucky. It was midweek, and there was only one drunk in the cell with him. At least the drunk was not sick. He did not really give a damn.

He was thinking of her. And David.

Eddie, a Friend
on the Force

Hearing voices, Johnny looked up through the bars, to hear another voice, a familiar voice that immediately lightened his mood. It was Eddie Landon, his best friend, arguing some formalities down the hall.

"Hey guys, what you doin? He needs to be wearing a white hat—he just saved about a hundred people. Come on…"

Good ol' Eddie, always there when you need him.

Eddie was a no-bullshit-kind of guy with both feet on the ground. Eddie Landon, 40 years old, broad-shouldered, balding, short, was but built like a Sherman tank. Where other people turned life into a knot of un-answerable questions, Eddie just plowed ahead and al-ways seemed to land on his feet, and always at least with half a smile.

But it had almost cost him his life…

They had met on the outskirts of Saigon, the evening before the final evacuation. Johnny had been assigned to a special task force—he never could remember why he joined the army. He was young then, and he wanted to be the best in something, and that was just what had come along. Eddie was not technically a ranger, because he had missed the physical qualification—something to do with bad hearing in one ear, but some colonel found his brash attitude inspiring and had pulled a few strings to get him on the mission.

For some reason, Johnny had figured Eddie might not make it through, so he had taken it upon himself to keep Eddie alive. He was right. When Eddie saw those four enemy soldiers about to kill that teenage girl he went berserk. He charged in without firing, using his rifle like a club, and bodies began flying. He did not have trouble with those four —it was the two who ran in from the back room with pistols in hand that were going to kill him.

But Johnny had been keeping a bead on that door, and neither of those men got more than six inches through before he put them down. He remembered their faces. He remembered the face of every man he had killed there...so many at close range...

Eddie finally appeared, jotting a note on a memo pad, like always.

Johnny was happy to see him.

Eddie motioned to the guard.

As the guards opened the cell, Johnny made a mental note not to kid Eddie about his weight. It was the one thing Eddie was sensitive about.

Eddie rolled in. "Not goin' too well, cap'n?"

Johnny tried to get up, then suddenly grabbed his side, wincing in pain.

Eddie rushed over to him, throwing Johnny's arm over his shoulder. Johnny smacked Eddie's memo pad with a disdainful flick of his wrist, ribbing him.

"Still wastin' trees, Eddie?"

Eddie chuckled. "Us mortals minds are still doin' it by the numbers. What'd these numb-nuts do to you—you look like shit."

"No coffee this morning," Johnny replied

"That stuff'll rust your pipes, cap'n," Eddie said.

Johnny smiled at the old lines he and Eddie had been tossing back and forth since they had known each other. Then, it all came back to him at once, with a force that made him shake and almost stumble. "That bomb woulda' taken out half the crowd, Eddie."

"I know, Cap'n...I know...I'm just takin' ya' home," Eddie said,

Johnny was glad someone understood. It made him feel just a little warmer inside.

They exited the cell and began walking down the corridor.

"Howdya' nail her? And don't tell me you dreamed her," Eddie asked.

Good ol' Eddie, knew the best possible thing he could do for him was to get him back on track. He was glad to go with it.

"I saw the real Kimono girl caught at some road-block on Second Avenue. Then I saw her double on the plaza, and the wire... "You gettin' on this case?"

"Naw, I saw you on television and I came down to get your autograph, whadiya' think? His sister called us last night about some death threats," Eddie tossed back.

"His sister?!" David had never told him he had sister, Johnny thought.

"Her name's Jessica. Guess she's been living in Europe, came back just a month ago. David never mentioned her? You must have seen her—she was still standin' over him when we arrived," Eddie said.

"That was his sister?! Jesus, who could miss her!" Johnny winced again. "She must be out of her mind after all this."

"You'd think so, wouldn't ya'," Eddie said. "But she wasn't. I tried talkin' to her—and whew—she was dead calm, like she was talking about something that happened in history a hundred years ago, you know what I mean?"

Johnny stopped, standing back, holding Eddie's shoulder to steady himself. His looked into Eddie's eyes.

Eddie knew what was coming.

"No way! No fuckin' way. Don't even think of askin'. Last time you did this to me...the last time..."

Johnny kept staring at him straight in the eye for all their friendship was worth.

"Work with me, Eddie," Johnny coaxed, "it'll be good for your career..."

Eddie shook his head slowly from side to side, not wanting to agree, knowing he was going to. "Aw, Jesus, "he muttered.

"Two days, Eddie, that's all I'm asking," Johnny continued.

"Come on, Johnny, this isn't special ops- we're not in charge here," Eddie said. "And why do you want to get all mixed up with this for, anyway?"

Johnny gave him a look. Only Eddie knew him in 'Nam, and only Eddie could talk to him about his time in the Phoenix Project. With anyone else, he did not want to remember, or ever think again about the things he had done.

Eddie continued, "Hye, really, Johnny, I just came down to get your ass out of the sling, not put mine in one."

"Eddie..." Johnny leaned on him.

Eddie kept protesting. "And whatdya' got me loanin' you money for your darkroom—you said you were done being a security jock."

Yeah, he was done, Johnny thought. He wanted to be done. But then again, he had never even thought of himself as one when he was doing it.

"I was backing him up, Eddie," Johnny said.

"David Ames?" Eddie, despite himself, was starting to get the picture.

Johnny hesitated, "He asked me to cover him today. "I was workin' for him, on and off, for two months...as a favor."

Eddie gave Johnny a look that told him he appreciated the professional honor at stake, and his friendship with David. "Jesus..."

Johnny held firm. "Two days, Eddie. Just work it with me."

"Shit," Eddie said, which Johnny knew meant yes, adding, "Just don't do anything to fuck me up with the Chief, Johnny..."

"You won't regret it, Eddie," Johnny said.

"I already regret it," Eddie complained.

Johnny broke away, turned and headed for the door. "I'm going to see Jessica Ames."

Eddie knew Johnny too well to be shocked with his lightning-like recovery. He just said, "Come see me after. You makin' her your first suspect?"

"My first witness," Johnny answered, walking through the door.

Eddie smirked and shouted after him. "Hey, what about your busted side!? And Christ, go home first and shower, you smell like a goddamn Sasquatch!"

Outside Johnny hailed a cab. He hopped in, and said, "Warehouse district. I'll tell you when to stop." Then he leaned back and closed his eyes, because he did not want to see any more of the city, any more of things outside, things he could not control. He just listened to the sounds of the tires on the road...

"Where to, pal?" The cab driver asked after a few minutes.

Johnny looked around to get his bearings.

"Let me off at the next light," Johnny said, and tossed a ten-dollar-bill over the seat. "Thanks."

The cab came to a stop, and he was back on the street again. He walked the half block to his building and decided to take the stairs up the six flights because he was already so damned tired.

Back in his studio, the radio was still on when he entered. He did not turn it off. Right now, he did not want any kind of silence. He emptied his keys and wallet down on the table. The photo of David he had developed last night was still there. The image hit him like a body blow. He hesitated, as the pain of David's loss shot through him again. He picked up the photo, tapping it lightly against the table, as he looked at his own reflection in one of the large windows.

The words the radio newscaster finally began reaching him.

"...a foiled assassination attempt culminated in a bizarre accident resulting in the death of prominent local businessman David Ames, current president of the Chilkat Corporation..."

He felt a slight breeze blowing his hair. He heard a window banging in the bathroom. He thought he had closed it.

With the photograph still in his hand, he entered the bathroom and walked over to the window. He leaned through it to look out—a construction crane had been mounted on the new skyscraper opposite his building. He closed the window, then latched it and unlatched it several times, wondering how it could have blown open. He stopped, confronted by his slightly warped reflection in the glass. Just another reflection, he thought, no two the same.

He walked back to the living room, picking up the torn portrait of Lara from the floor...He checked his thoughts as he had done a thousand times before. No time for that. He had something to do. He owed it to David, and to himself. He stripped down and stepped into the shower to wash off the sweat and blood.

The Woman in the Tower

An hour later, now clean-shaven, and well-groomed, Johnny found himself back on the Chilkat Tower plaza, attired in a white dress shirt, navy blue sport coat, and pressed, dark blue jeans. The plaza was empty, the crowds long since dispersed.

He stood at the death site, looking down at a few blood-stained leaves and a blood-spotted piece of silver gum wrapper. The pool of blood and blood spray has already been scrubbed and cleaned. He stooped to lift one of the leaves a few inches from the pavement, turning it back and forth to examine it. He looked toward the seventeenth floor, then slowly around the plaza, taking it all in.

Across the street, twenty stories up, a crane worked atop the rising steel frame of a new skyscraper. He dropped the leaf and walked toward the main entrance.

The guard at the front desk directed him to where he wanted to go. He stood in front of two glass doors, taking a moment to read the stenciled letters, "Paul Erickson - Head of Security - Chilkat Corporation."

He looked through the letters on the glass door to appraise the man sitting behind the desk inside, and then entered. The man who stood to greet him was polished and professional.

"Yes?" he said.

"I'm Johnny Hammond. I'm working with the Seattle P.D. on the investigation," Johnny said, stretching the truth.

"I know who you are," Erickson responded coolly.

So that's the way it was going to be, Johnny thought.

"Then let's not waste each other's time," Johnny replied. "I've got a few questions. You can answer them now, or you can answer them downtown. One phone call. You decide."

Erickson did not respond to the bluff. "If I had anything I thought was important, I'd tell you," Erickson said, defending his turf.

"Sure, you would. For now, I just want to know who has been in the building," Johnny said.

"Nobody interesting," Erickson stated flatly.

"Nobody interesting?" Johnny paused and gazed at him. "No subcontractors, repairmen, anybody?"

"Nobody interesting, "Erickson repeated, surveying him. "The logs are clear for a month. And the employees all wear picture I.D.'s. We've got a monitor on every entrance and elevator, and infrared motion sensors on every empty floor."

"Check the ledger three months back," Johnny said. "Who screens your employees?" Johnny asked. "You're not outsourced on that, are you?"

Erickson stood his ground. "Chilkat Corporation could put people in missile silos."

Johnny shot him a sideways glance. "I wouldn't know––is that good?"

He didn't wait for an answer. "I'll need access to the videos for the seventeenth floor."

"Miss Ames ordered no materials be released," Erickson said.

Obstacles every step of the way, and it seemed like Jessica Ames was putting them there. "Miss Ames? When'd she take over? And what about William, or Mark?"

"You'll have to ask her, "Erickson responded coolly.

"I will," Johnny promised. "You know, Erickson, you don't seem to have a lot of loyalty to the man that was writing your paycheck. How long have you been here, or is that confidential, too?"

"I've been here a year, and as for David Ames, I never really knew the man," Erickson said.

"Is that a fact?" Johnny started to leave. "Erickson, I have a feeling I'm going to be seeing you again. Think about taking some singing lessons."

For a moment, Johnny and Erickson locked eyes. Then Johnny turned and exited abruptly. There was always once simple theory he had followed in private investigation: pursue the path of most resistance. If someone is laying down the red carpet for you, it is probably because they are showing you out the door.

He walked down the hall to the elevator lobby, pressed the call button. Still, things were moving fast, much too fast. He would miss something if he was not careful. The elevator bell rang, the doors opened, and he got on.

He let his eyes roam around the elevator as it climbed. There was something here, too. But nothing visible to the eyes. He felt it in the walls. The whole corporation reeked of it. He had expected some basic cooperation from Erickson.

He was not sure what it was he had gotten, but he would not forget it.

The elevator came to a stop, and he walked out onto a bare concrete floor, toward two policemen, Patrick Dolan, Eddie's new partner, and Paul Valenti. You couldn't forget Patrick, loyal to the bone, third generation Boston Irish cop come to Seattle, as Irish as they come, 28, tall, lanky, always sporting a real smile. Paul Valenti was another story. He didn't like Johnny, and Johnny didn't like him.

Valenti stepped in front of him, blocking his way.

"Going to take some pretty pictures, Hammond?" he scoffed.

Johnny violently grabbed his throat. "Bastard!" Pushed him against the wall.

Patrick broke them apart.

"Hey! Hey! Lighten up, Johnny!" Patrick turned to Valenti. "Back off, Paul, will you?"

Johnny walked on by, nodding to Patrick, "Patrick..." He and Valenti had run into each other on another investigation. Valenti had come out of it looking pretty stupid. It was not Johnny's fault. He had just been doing his job. But now he was in no mood for jokes about David's death.

Patrick called after him. "Hold on to something—the wind's blowing like a mother."

"Right," Johnny tossed back over his shoulder. What the Hell else could he do, he thought.

Johnny walked down a corridor, and turned onto a vast empty floor, with only a few aluminum stud walls standing on the cement. On the far wall of glass, the horizon was visible through a 10 x 16-foot hole, the floor-to-ceiling hole where the window had blown out. It was covered with an "X" of yellow police tape, rippling in the wind.

Standing a few feet back, he looked out through the opening to the sky, as the wind gusted outside. He approached the frame cautiously, taking hold, and ran his finger down the empty metal frame, checking for dust. Nothing—the metal frame was evenly pushed out, with no visible marks. He stepped toward the edge. Taking a firm grip on the window frame, he leaned over and peered through, careful to maintain his balance and stay out of the wind.

"You win some and you lose some, don't you, Mr. Hammond?" The voice behind him was silky, but somber and intense.

Johnny turned, shocked by the words, more shocked when he recognized the woman standing there as the one he had seen on the plaza, Jessica Ames. Damn, she was attractive, much too attractive.

"Jessica Ames," she introduced herself, "I'm sorry if that sounded harsh. David thought very highly of you."

Johnny said nothing as she approached him in her perfectly tailored and pressed pantsuit.

She stopped, adding, "And I'm sure he still would...were he still alive."

Johnny caught the double meaning. Who the Hell was this woman? And where did she fit in?

"I knew your brother a lot of years, Miss Ames."

Jessica strolled past him to the open window, running a finger along the inner frame.

"I only knew him when I was very young." A moment passed as they regarded one another. "Do you enjoy your work, Mr. Hammond?"

"Photography's very rewarding, Miss Ames." He was not about to give her anything.

She caught his tact immediately and eyed him critically. "A photographer without a camera? And David thought you were involved with security."

"I was," Johnny said.

"But no longer?" she queried.

"No..." Was he, or wasn't he? He hardly knew himself now. "It was a terrible accident..." he said, not knowing what else to say.

A moment of silence passed between them, as she stared at him. She did not like what he had said. "...a terrible accident," she echoed him. "...no longer involved with security..." She surveyed him with a cool arrogance as lord and judge. "When I got the message in Paris after all these years that David needed me to come immediately, I thought, 'but he must be surrounded by competent people.' Apparently not." Then she turned and began walking away, only stopping momentarily to toss a remark over her shoulder.

"And do you still believe in the tooth fairy, Mr. Hammond?" she asked seriously and continued walking away.

Her words hit a nerve. What was it? A sense of guilt, not wanting to face that he might have been able to do something to save David if he had arrived on time? No, it was more than that, but what? Not catching himself, he uttered something after her...

"Let's stick something under your pillow and see what happens." What the hell was that? He was letting this woman get under his skin.

She left.

He decided to follow her to her office. He took the elevator to the penthouse on the forty-eighth floor. The doors opened upon a beautiful eighteen-year-old receptionist sitting behind a desk.

"Hello, I'm Johnny Hammond, for Miss Ames. And you are?"

She smiled flatly. "Do you have an appointment, Mr. Hammond?"

Johnny leaned over her desk. "I suggest you ask Miss Ames," he said, reading her desk plate to add, "Jamie."

A door opened silently. Jessica stood in the doorway, observing and overhearing.

"I need to speak with her about your security systems," Johnny said.

They both sensed Jessica's presence at the same time, looking up to see her smiling over them. She appeared, startlingly fresh, innocent, childlike.

"Careful, Jamie, he's good with a gun," Jessica quipped.

Johnny watched as Jessica's attention was momentarily drawn away by a mother and daughter, passing hand in hand in the corridor, and saw a strange expression pass over her face.

Then she pivoted and disappeared back into her office.

Johnny was getting used to her strange comments. He let it pass and glanced at the open door of her office. He entered.

Jessica had taken a seat behind a massive modern black metal frame and glass desk, sitting in a formal posture with her hands folded before her on her desk.

He approached, glancing behind her to an oil portrait on the wall of the company president, a handsome Caucasian man in his forties, affixed with a small brass plate, 'Austin Ames.'

She saw him looking at and said, "My biological father. Never knew him. He died a few months after I was born." Then she spoke directly. "You're not with law enforcement. Why are you here? Who are you working for?"

So, this is the way it was going to be. "Why am I here? Why are you here? And where's William, or Itomi and his people?"

She just looked at him, deciding to respond to his earlier, unspoken question. "I am here because this corporation is now mine. The portrait is of Austin Ames." She paused. "They say he was some kind of genius. He had all the security systems installed. I don't even know who is running them now. You will have to talk to Paul Erickson."

He would have to watch his balance if he was going to follow all the curves in this road. "Yeah, had a great talk with him."

"So that's it, then...." she replied coolly.

"David never showed me any pictures of your father," Johhny said casually, hoping for more information.

She was staring at him, sizing him up. "Any more questions, Mr. Hammond?"

He had not really asked any. He regarded her. "One, for now. You always get what you want, Miss Ames?"

"So now you're 'investigating' as well?" she shot back at him.

"You mean besides killing," Johnny said.

"You seemed good at it," she said matter-of-factly.

It stopped Johnny. He had no answer.

"So, tell me what you saw on the seventeenth floor," she answered.

Johnny looked at her, not knowing which way he should go with her. He decided not to take her into his confidence. "I'm sure the police department will keep you informed of anything they find out."

Jessica pushed an envelope across the desk, then waited for him to reach for it.

"Need something mailed?" Johnny asked without missing a beat.

She was not amused. "Ten thousand dollars, Mr. Hammond. A retainer. You can work for me."

"You've been expecting me," Johnny said.

"I always plan ahead," she said in her best executive tone.

"So, what exactly do you want to buy, Miss Ames?" he asked.

"The truth, of course," she said.

Johnny just stared at her. What was behind her crisp, polished manner? He had come in on a gut feeling, and that feeling was growing stronger. He decided to just stand there looking at her.

She returned the envelope to the drawer, and gave him a luminous smile...that smile, it could make a man forget where he was. She was a cool one, he thought. Maybe she even knew how to run the corporation better than her two remaining brothers.

"You know, <u>Johnny</u>..." she said, emphasizing his name with distinct pronunciation, "...making me a suspect could interfere with our friendship."

"I don't think so," Johnny answered flatly.

Jessica smiled. "I'll take that as a compliment. Now tell me about the seventeenth floor," she insisted.

All right, he would tell her, but just the obvious. "A strong wind, altitude, air pressure variants, possible spontaneous decompression—looks like an accident."

Jessica stood, suddenly peeved. "Of course, it looks like an accident! It always looks like an accident. A battlefield looks like an accident!"

Johnny was not taken aback, more fascinated than disturbed by her outburst. Fiery temperaments in women had always fascinated him. He thought it showed a range and a capacity for passion and experience. He observed her as she made a show of recomposing herself, straightening her jacket, and smoothing her sleeves.

"I mean you won't find anything, Mr. Hammond. Because there is nothing to find." She sat back down, hitting the intercom. "Jamie."

Johnny stood. "I need the videos from the security cameras."

"I'll have them sent," she retorted.

Jamie entered.

"Jamie, Mr. Hammond is looking for a way out." She turned to Johnny. "Excuse me."

Johnny watched her disappear behind a mahogany door.

With an air of protectiveness, Jamie addressed him. "Perhaps another time would be better, Mr. Hammond."

Johnny fixed his eyes on the mahogany door. He heard the sound of running water from a faucet. He turned toward Jamie. Where had Jessica found her?

"Sure." Sure, he thought. What did it matter? He was not getting anywhere with her, or least not here, not now. Every time he pushed in one direction, something pushed back...must mean he was on the right track.

Johnny left the building and decided to walk the ten blocks to the police station. Maybe it would help him clear his mind a little. Start again...

It was late at night when he walked through the set of double glass doors reading "Seattle Police Department - Homicide Division." As he stepped in, he looked back to see the rain just beginning to wet the pavement.

Eddie was waiting for him. "You get the tapes, Johnny?"

Maybe he had not done so well. "She's sending them."

"She's sending them? What, like C.O.D.? Material evidence, Johnny. It only counts when it's in your hand. Don't worry, I already got them."

"Alright, before your head swells any larger, Eddie, what's her story?"

Eddie grabbed his notepad. "Thought you'd never ask. The bylaws have a sole survivor clause for the family. She just inherited all David's stock in the Chilkat Corporation... about three-hundred and twenty-one million dollars. Tellya' anything?"

"She's rich?" Johnny quipped.

"You're a genius, Johnny," Eddie said.

"Yeah, I try to keep up...so what? I'm sure it was originally divided three ways, with David and Mark. So why wasn't David's share split with Mark? And what about Itomi? You ever think about him?" Johnny asked.

"Come on, Johnny, David didn't have any enemies! Itomi's back in Tokyo and you're going out of your way to avoid the obvious. This land thing's been goin' on for years. Everything was fine until little Miss Muffet came along."

"So, you've got Jessica Ames in your sights? Forget it. I looked in her eyes. Money's not what she's about, Eddie." He knew that would get him.

Eddie framed Johnny with his fingers. "Hold that pose...I'm hearing the theme music from the Twilight Zone."

"You really don't like her," Johnny said.

"I don't like what's inside her. I can't put my finger on it, but she's no little Red Riding Hood, fuckin' beautiful or not," Eddie said. "And she is twenty-eight-year-old. Perfect time to think about money."

"Reading a lot of fairy tales, lately, or what? Why don't you just give her a break, she's just trying to hold together," Johnny said.

"You're just hoppin' along in fairyland, Johnny. I wonder if you'd be coverin' for her if she didn't look like Miss America."

"I'm thinking more Miss France," Johnny replied.

Eddie handed Johnny the file. "I'd take a look at this if I were you. Double master's in psychology, chemical engineering."

Johnny picked up the file. "And?"

Eddie continued, "So I say to you, son, leave it alone, she'll eat you for breakfast."

"Criminals don't eat breakfast," Johnny said. He could not think of anything else to say.

Eddie smirked. "That girl could sit in your lap even when you're standin' up.

Just don't come crying to me when she nails your butt to the ceiling."

"I can handle it. I can handle her," Johnny said.

"Sure..." Eddie grabbed a bulletproof armor vest, threw it to Johnny.

"For those romantic evenings, then."

Johnny caught it, turning it over to see the small skull-and-crossbones painted on each side of the chest.

"Nice. But not really my color," Johnny said.

Eddie shook his head, punching up a video on the screen. "We got this from WKLR. Not public." The monitor showed the woman on the plaza being shot, recovering, being shot again. "Coke or meth might do that, but she came up clean on the autopsy," Eddie said.

"Hypnosis?" Johnny offered.

"Maybe. Or you'd think she had to be on something. We're running her prints now, and I sent a photo to the state department. We know one thing—she's native American, not Asian. They're still working on the bomb pack she was carrying. Now look, lab boys never seen the likes." Eddie pointed to the screen. "Some kind of massive force on this window frame, but it's not twisted. And the spectrometer came up blank for explosive trace."

"That possible?" Johnny asked.

"Not by anything we know—shoulda' left some trace," Eddie said. "If it was a concussion from a charge set farther away, it woulda' blown out more than one frame or at least shattered it. But get this." Eddie hit the start button again, showing the huge pane of glass rushing down, then he re-wound it again, slowing it down, to reveal the glass falling intact above David's head— Johnny turned away— slicing through his body.

"All one piece—shit—sorry, Johnny."

"Yeah..."

Eddie continued. "Bizarre, huh? And nobody heard a thing. I asked the building engineers about wind pressure and all that technical bullshit."

Johnny, his back now turned, looked out the window, feeling the loss of his friend, remembering their times together.

Eddie did not notice.

Johnny turned back, steeling himself to go on. "Play the crowd part back... No, the VIP part... yeah... That's strange, William and Itomi backing up like that..."

Eddie countered, "Engineers said no way. No way you could ever time or target something so near where he was standing—no human agent possible, that's what they said."

The phone rang and Eddie picked it up. "Landon...yeah." A look of surprise came over Eddie's face. He handed the phone to Johnny. "It's for you."

Curious, Johnny took the phone." I didn't tell anybody—" and then into the phone, "...hello?"

"Am I interrupting you, Johnny?" the voice asked. It was Jessica.

"No, don't worry about it." Johnny looked to Eddie as he spoke into the phone.

"I thought it might be nice to see each other tonight," she said softly.

"What did you have in mind?" Johnny asked, going with it. It seemed he had been right to contact her. He was ready for the ride.

"A little something to eat. You know Canlis?" she asked.

David must have taken her there, he thought. "Yeah, I know it. When?"

She just said, "See you there, Johnny. Eight."

The phone hung up.

Johnny shrugged. "Jessica Ames just invited me out to dinner."

"Don't end up on the plate," Eddie quipped.

Johnny thought for a moment. "You think the window was an accident?"

"If it wasn't, we're sure as hell dancin' with the devil," Eddie answered, and then paused, seeing the other thought behind Johnny's question. "You couldn't have done anything, Johnny, and you're just beating yourself up if you think otherwise."

"I wonder, Eddie..." He had to say it, had to let it out. He started to leave.

"Johnny..." Eddie said, holding up the armor vest.

"Yeah, yeah..." Johnny took it from his hand, and walked out to his car. He threw the armor vest through the half-open back window into the back seat. Three hundred restaurants in the city and she had to pick that one. Where he had last seen Lara. At least he was still swimming in the right direction, upstream, against the current.

Ten minutes later, in front of Canlis, the valet was driving away his beaten-up Ford Explorer. He entered and approached the hostess desk. The restaurant was elegant and dim.

"Hi...I'm wondering if a Jessica Ames has been seated?"

The hostess shook her head. "No, but your table is ready. Follow me."

"Right," Johnny nodded.

She took two menus and brought Johnny to a quiet table near a large dark window. "Your waiter will be right with you," she said and left. The busboy filled the glasses with water and left.

Johnny sipped the water, watching the headlights of cars passing on the other side of the wall of dark-tinted windows. The cars would approach from around a far bend, the beams of their headlights swinging around to flash into the restaurant before passing by. As each car passed, the window would grow momentarily dark, so that he could see his face in the glass. His mind drifted.

The waiter had come and gone three times. He looked at his watch. An hour had passed. Still no sign of Jessica. The busboy approached.

"Another glass of water, sir?"

Johnny did not hear him.

"Lot of traffic today," the busboy offered.

Johnny noticed the kindness. "Yeah, thanks, I'm good."

Johnny kept watching the door.

The phone rang. The hostess answered but did not look to him. He threw a five-dollar bill down and walked out. It was still raining.

He gave another five to the parking valet. The meal was not filling, but the price was right.

Johnny reached his loft an hour later. He unlocked the door and entered, turning back to lock the door behind himself. He heard something. He spun around and listened. He heard sounds from the kitchen. He pulled his gun and cautiously approached. Then he saw her.

Jessica stood at the counter, calmly mixing cocktails with one hand, as she occasionally looked at the marred photograph of Lara she held in her other hand.

She turned toward him, glass in hand. "On the rocks or straight up? I had to guess."

Johnny looked around cautiously as he moved toward her, so the counter remained between them. "How did you get in here?"

"I didn't climb through the window." She waved the photo. "What did this white woman do to you, Johnny?"

Johnny walked over to her, taking the photo from her hand. "I take it you weren't hungry."

She smiled coyly in mock seduction." Hmm, you are a detective."

"You want to tell me what you're doing here?" he asked again.

"Helping you out..." She handed him a drink. "You can't seem to decide whether to fuck me or fingerprint me." She said it casually, like a statement of fact. Then she laughed, nodding toward a box on the floor. "I brought you the tapes."

"I already saw the dupes," he said.

Jessica, business-like, pulled an envelope from her purse, dropped it down onto the counter between them. "But not this. You might find our corporation a little unusual in some ways," she said.

"You mean being native American owned?" He waited for her reaction but got none. "In the 1930's your grandmother was the ancestral leader of her tribe, one of the largest Native American owned land tracts in the state. Your mother became the tribal elder when your grandmother died. Your father, half Native American, built a corporation by convincing her to sell it off piece by piece and herding the three hundred Indian families living there into a smaller and smaller corner..."

"Whatever you may know, or think you know..." she tried to interrupt.

He continued. "The proceeds were supposed to go into a trust fund for the tribe, but..."

"You don't know this," she finished her sentence, withdrawing a report from the envelope. "I pulled it from the corporation's files for you. It's a confidential report on the Bremerton land—page three you may find of interest."

Johnny accepted the report from her hand and opened it. He began flipping through the pages, reading silently, then aloud. "...the three remaining tribal elders present no more than a publicity problem. The ground, according to superstition, is protected by a curse, rumored..." He looked up, then continued, "...to be the cause of three deaths and one insanity after an attempt in 1971 by company chairman Austin Ames to sell the land and relocate the inhabitants."

Johnny looked up to see Jessica staring at him. What was her game? He was not about to give her the satisfaction. "Curse? Like the gods are angry?" He said it without due respect, and she noticed.

"My father was the first to die, Mr. Hammond," she said icily. "August 1971. Along with a coastal commissioner who was supporting his plan, and a BLM agent who wasn't. You know, I hate what my brothers are doing, but they certainly don't deserve to die for it."

"I'm sorry." He really was. He continued on a more conciliatory note. "You believe one of these elders might be involved in your brother's murder?"

"You do intend to conduct a thorough investigation, don't you?" She did not wait for his answer. "My brother is dead, in an assassination plot of which you apparently had foreknowledge-"

"Foreknowledge?!" Johnny protested.

She glared back. "Will you let me finish?!" She stopped, this time waiting for his acknowledgement before continuing. "However it was accomplished, I want you to find, and preferably kill the bastards, who obviously wish to appear as the avenging angels of this curse. The color of the robes they may be wearing, whether they can walk through walls or how high they can fly does not concern me, nor am I in the least interested in the limited horizon of your adopted Caucasian prejudice." She stepped toward him, standing straight and hard, face to face. "I know what color your blood runs, Johnny Hammond." Now she locked her eyes with his. "The four deaths surrounding the last violation—"

"Four?" Johnny interrupted.

"—occurred every twelve hours. David died at eleven twenty-two this morning."

"Who else knows about this? Where are your brothers?" he asked.

"I guess we'll be finding out, won't we?" She checked her watch. "It's ten o'clock, Mr. Hammond. What are you going to do?" Jessica turned and left, slipping quickly through the door.

Johnny stood staring at the door for a moment, then checked his watch. He took a moment to read again the passage in the report concerning the Curse. Everything told him not to believe it, but he could not put it from his mind.

He picked up the phone, pressing the speed-dial.

"Eddie? Listen—"

"How was dinner?" Eddie asked. "You keepin' your mind right, Johnny?"

"We ended up at my place," Johnny said.

"Your place?!" Eddie asked, startled.

"She just left," Johnny said.

There was a pause on the other end of the line. "I hope you're keepin' it under wraps," Eddie said. "...what'd ya' find out?"

"I'm just giving her some rope," Johnny answered, "but I need you to check the newspapers for some unexplained deaths in Bremerton...and a list of people who have access to the corporate records at the Chilkat Corporation."

"Okay, Johnny. But just remember, the clock's runnin'," Eddie advised.

"In more ways than you know—wait——and Austin Ames' will, if he left one—and whoever came before him. We need to find out who really owns this corporation, and who controls it."

Johnny hung up.

Once again, he looked at the document in his hand. He tossed it down and went to the sink to get a drink of water. Then he returned to stare at the document, captured by its pronouncement despite himself. He could not tell how many moments had passed when he finally shook himself from its spell, and retired to his bed, to his dreams...

He was waking up...into a candlelit bedroom not his own.... a dark figure was approaching the foot of the bed. A flash of heat lightning threw the figure into black silhouette...

Johnny woke suddenly, sitting up, staring at the foot of his bed. He could hear rain hitting his windows. The room was dark and empty, but he could feel sweat on his forehead. Death was too close, all around.

The First Sighting

Out on the highway, the storm was growing worse. Wind-driven rain lashed the corporate silver limousine of William Ames, forcing the driver to slow to a crawl. A line of cars barely moved in front of them.

William was on the car phone, arguing with Jessica, as the limousine approached a stopped line of cars up ahead. "A couple of years?! How can you say that?! Who knows when those two are going to their happy hunting grounds?! We're talking about a hundred million dollars, Jessie! For Chrissakes, get some perspective!" He yelled to the driver, "What the hell is going on up there?!

"What time is it?" He continued with Jessica. "I'm at the West Seattle Bridge."

"I'll be there in ten minutes. Just wait. And start thinking about it," William said.

"Eleven twenty-one," the driver responded.

"Son-of-a-bitch. Son-of-a-bitch," William intoned.

The limousine horn began honking, as the wind blasted through the tall trees lining the roadside.

Johnny's phone rang in his loft. He turned over but did not awaken. The phone kept ringing. Finally, he picked it up. "Hello?" But there was no answer, only a high wind and static, transmitted by a cellular phone. He dropped the phone back into the cradle and fell back to sleep.

Out on the highway, William opened the limousine door and stepped partially out, craning his neck to find the cause of the traffic jam.

Violent gusts of wind exploded all around him. Branches and scraps of cardboard flailed against the car.

"Fucking wind." William said, stepping out of the car.

Then he heard a snap. It came at him a black whip too fast to see. The broken power line whipped down and around his neck and torso, dancing over his body like an angry snake. An arc of blue light burned all around him as he convulsed and screamed horribly in a macabre dance of death, even louder than the roaring of the wind.

Johnny's phone rang again. He rolled over still half asleep and put the receiver to his ear. There was screaming, horrible screaming, on and on, until the line suddenly disconnected. He looked at the clock by the phone. 11:22 PM. He clicked the telephone receiver several times—it was dead. He dropped the phone back into the cradle, thinking to get up but a massive weight was descending on him. His limbs were turning to stone, and the arms of dreams were reaching up to pull him back from the passageway of near waking.

In her office, Jessica's face froze, as she listened to the sound of William's screaming over the car phone. Too many thoughts and emotions were colliding within her. In a near trance, she hung up, and walked across her office, through the mahogany door, partially closing it behind her. After a moment, the quiet office filled with the sound of a faucet turning on, and of running water.

At the accident scene, police cars, fire trucks, and public utility vehicles flashed their multi-colored lights through the rain. A large crowd of onlookers encircled two emergency medical technicians as they zipped up a black body bag.

Overhead, a worker in a lift bucket examined a transformer atop a telephone pole, and shouted down, "Son-of-a-bitch burned clean thru'. But the lines are testing clear!"

"Test 'em again," the man on the ground shouted back, trying to make himself heard over the storm.

An Unexpected Visitor

Johnny was sleeping when the door buzzer awakened him. He rolled out of bed, not quite leaving his dreams, throwing on his pants and shirt, and went to the intercom. "Eddie, that you?"

There was no answer. He struck the intercom with the heel of his hand, not sure it was working. He pressed it again. "Hang on, I'm coming down."

A moment later, down on the ground floor, he opened the door.

She stood at his doorstep in the rain. He watched the drops run down her perfectly sculpted features, over her lips. She seemed fragile, and lost. He wanted to kiss her.

But she spoke first, with ominous tone.

"Your phone is disconnected," she said.

He hardly heard her; he only knew he was glad she was there. How could he tell her?

The moment passed, and he only answered groggily. "I know. You working for the phone company now?" He knew he had said the wrong thing.

Jessica slipped past him through the doorway with a remark, "That shirt's not a good color on you," and drifted in, as into her own home, taking off her coat and scarf, observing herself in his entrance hall mirror.

"It's cold tonight. Were you cold?" she asked.

He forced himself back to the mundane, not sure whether he had just glimpsed something more. Now he just looked at her, wondering what she was doing there, where it might lead. "I don't think so," he lied. He was always cold now.

"Sometimes my fingers are freezing and I'm indoors. Circulation, they say." She suddenly laughed, delighted, like a child. "Cold hands, warm heart."

Johnny forced himself to observe, and concentrate.

"Do you want something hot, some tea or coffee?" he asked.

"No..." She hesitated. She looked to him as if seeking his approval for what she was about to say. "...my brothers are against me, you know. They're all against me."

Johnny looked at her, surprised and caught by her revelation.

Jessica sat down, taking off her shoes as she spoke.

"William doesn't know how much I could give the company, if he'd just give me the chance..." She paused again. "I have two degrees."

She was speaking as though she did not control everything in the corporation. But her thought stopped there. She shook her head, as though she were so tired nothing really mattered any more. "I'm so tired...I need to rest, Johnny."

She found her way to his bed, curling up on top of the covers.

Johnny just stared at her. The phone began ringing. Jessica froze. Johnny, startled, moved toward it, watching her, wondering what lay ahead.

"No!" Jessica blurted out. "Don't answer it!"

Johnny stopped, not understanding.

"Please." She was visibly frightened. Without thinking, she began unbuttoning her blouse, then just as suddenly, she stopped, as though not remembering what she was doing.

"I need to stay here tonight," she announced. Then, without waiting for a response, she slipped under the covers, curling up into a ball, facing away from him.

Johnny hesitated at the phone. It stopped ringing. He looked back to her as she was falling asleep. He lit a candle, turned off the lights, and approached her. She slept like a child, on her side, hands cupped together in front of her lips. For a long time, he stood over her, listening to her breathing.

He knew it was as close as he would ever come to truly seeing her, or into that world that she wore like a cloak. Who knew whether it was a world he would ever know, or even ever want to know? With any other woman, at any other time, it would have been enough that she was near now. But he had to go deeper, for the investigation. He wanted it and needed it. He lit a candle and turned down the lights. Then he sat back against the arm of his couch, swinging his legs up. Soon he was drifting in and out of sleep.

The candle, burning low, was the only light in the room. His dreams were rich, coaxing memories and voices from shadowed places, all marching, marching somewhere in the night.

Jessica awoke, bolted upright to a sitting position and gasped, staring into the space above the foot of the bed. "No!" she cried. "Nooo!"

Johnny woke up, looked to Jessica, and quickly looked around, to be sure they were alone.

"What's is it?" he asked. For a moment, Jessica remained frozen, not answering. "...a nightmare?" Johnny offered.

Jessica threw off the covers, got out of the bed, "I don't like candles," she said.

Johnny reached over and turned on the lamp.

Jessica walked to the window, pressing her face close to the screen to draw some clear breaths of the outside air. She spoke half to herself.

"I don't like candles," she said again.

"I'll leave the light on." He moved to her, next to her. He saw now her eyes were red, and that she had been crying. He reached out to touch her shoulder. Jessica drew back and froze, glaring at him.

"I thought I could trust you," she said bitterly.

Johnny looked at her. "What?!"

Jessica looked around as though concerned with her safety, plotting a way to the door as she grabbed her coat and hurriedly threw it on.

"I am going," she repeated, as though entranced.

Johnny followed her to the door.

"Jessica...." It was all so wrong. He thought he could embrace her and comfort her, but she was leaving, disturbed and frightened.

Jessica opened the door and stepped outside. Suddenly she turned and embraced him, then broke away. She hurried out, toward a waiting black limousine. His phone rang and he stepped back inside the hall.

"Hello," he said, still peering out through the door.

No answer. He dropped the phone. He looked back out toward the street. A different limousine, white, was pulling toward the bottom of the steps. A loud off-the-hook signal started bleeping on the phone—he picked it up and replaced the receiver. It at once began ringing again. He let it ring as he watched the chauffeur open the door for her. Strangely, she kissed him on the lips before she got in. He walked back to the phone and picked it up. The limousine drove off.

"Yeah?" he inquired again.

"Johnny, it's Eddie."

"Eddie," Johnny said.

"Johnny, William Ames is dead."

"What?" But Johnny had heard him perfectly.

"He's dead, Johnny," Eddie said.

Johnny knew he was dead. He had to be dead. "How?" he asked. Did it matter?

"Power line. Electrocuted," Eddie said.

Johnny remembered the screaming on the phone. "Christ. When, Eddie?"

"Around eleven-thirty," Eddie answered.

"Exactly, Eddie, exactly," Johnny pressed.

"Eleven twenty-two," Eddie said. "His watch stopped then."

Johnny, stunned, said nothing. Impossible, but it had happened. He had died exactly twelve hours after David. He looked down at the report still on his table. The Curse? He was suddenly nauseous.

"Johnny? ...Johnny? You there?" Eddie said anxiously.

Johnny hit the speakerphone button, paused, and walked over to the window to look out, as though in a trance, "I'm here."

"Johnny? This has got to be a family thing, comin' or goin'—we've got to question Jessica and Mark Ames. And the sooner the better. This is starting to look like some kind of vendetta against the whole family."

"It's okay, she was here," Johnny said, knowing nothing he could say would explain it to Eddie.

"Jessica Ames? Jessica Ames, Johnny? Jesus, Johnny, Jesus," Eddie confronted him.

"She was scared. She doesn't know anyone here, she just showed up," Johnny said.

There was a pause, and Eddie asked, "You fuck her? Did you fuck her, Johnny?"

Eddie knew him better than that. Why was he saying that? "No. She came back," Johnny said distractedly.

"Back? What? What do you mean, came back? You're not making any sense."

Johnny knew he was not making any sense.

"Talk to me, Johnny," Eddie continued. "You goin' off on one of your obsessions, Johnny?"

Johnny stared out the window, as though his thoughts might follow her trail into the night. "You gotta' let me go with this one, Eddie," was all he could say. This storm was not going to let him out. He had to find a way through.

"What are you talkin' about, Johnny?" Eddie was incredulous. "You flippin' out on me, Johnny? That's two down, two to go. You gonna' wait to see who's left standing?! You think this is some fuckin' video game?" Eddie was nearly shouting.

"I got it covered, Eddie. Look, I had some trouble with my phone. I need to know when it started," Johnny said.

Silence on the other end of the line. "Hear me? Eddie? I got it covered," Johnny said into the phone, but his words just seemed to echo back to him from the vast space inside himself.

The silence grew longer. "Eddie?" Still no answer...

Finally, Eddie answered. "You better hang on for the ride then, Romeo..."

"Eddie, the facts..." Johnny shot back.

"No record of trouble," Eddie answered. "I checked when I couldn't reach you. Between repair service and me, we must have tried you ten times between eleven and eleven-thirty..."

Now Johnny froze. That crack into that other world opened into a yawning chasm.

Eddie continued, "...it just kept ringing."

Johnny, silent, looked around the room. "Johnny? You okay, Johnny? ...You want me to come out?" Eddie's voice came from the mouthpiece, but Johnny was already holding the phone away from his ear, looking out the window.

Then he recovered. "No, Eddie, I'll meet you there."

"A mile out from the Westlake Bridge. You'll see it," Eddie said.

"Right." Johnny hung up.

Suddenly the wind again blew open one of the windows. He walked over to them, again examined the latch. As he was about to close it, he was again stopped by his own reflection. What was there, and what only appeared to be there. Somewhere in between there was a doorway into her world.

On Its Tracks

Johnny arrived at the accident scene twenty minutes later, pulling his car up to the yellow police ribbons.

The yellow, red, and blue lights of the police cars, ambulances, and utility vehicles painted an ever-changing kaleidoscope of color through the light drizzle. Electricity crackled and shorted, emitting occasional bursts of illuminating blue light that cast an eerie pallor upon the faces of the crowd. The wind whipped and exploded into the dull emptiness of the grim tasks borne by the civil servants.

He spotted Eddie, as always, scribbling notes.

"Hey Eddie," he said in a somber, even tone, by which he meant to convey his respect for the dead.

Eddie looked up from his pad and nodded in acknowledgment. "Not much left."

Johnny took in the scene. As with any other accident, the police controlled the scene, the medical technicians made their reports, the utility workers set about their repairs. It was too ordinary. So ordinary, he could feel the protest rising up inside him. They were sweeping up death, hosing it down, covering the lies, forgetting, disappearing.

Did only he feel the judgement that had been executed here? And who, or what, was the executioner? Reigning from a realm above or below? Was it laughing now at this grim efficiency that restored the illusion of order to this world and made its terrible violation invisible? Made its existence and motive not suspect?

Johnny looked up at the power lines, still blowing in the wind like the tendrils of some unknown life. At that moment, his investigation split into the two worlds he saw appearing before him, where others would see only one. That other world, that deadly world, he would enter alone, even while following a course more understandable to all around him. "Eddie, talk to the power guys yet?" he said simply.

"One of 'em," Eddie said, scribbling on his pad.

"Wind blow down a line?" Johnny asked.

"It wasn't the wind, Johnny. The line melted right through for no reason. They can't figure it," Eddie said.

Something about the way Eddie said it struck him.

"Another freak accident, you think?" Eddie said.

"Maybe...," Johnny echoed his words, "...another freak accident..."

Eddie lifted his eyes from his pad momentarily, looking at Johnny.

Johnny walked toward the utility pole. He hoped beyond all hope it might be proved an accident, but he spoke his mind, quoting Jessica from memory, "...Do you still believe in the tooth fairy?"

"What?" Eddie asked.

"Jessica said it. Maybe it's a way in." Every child knew or soon learned it was a mother of father that put money under their pillow...but it was a borderline no one pressed too hard, leaving a no man's land between the real and the imagined, the fanciful...but Johnny said nothing more. He was too absorbed in reading and feeling the signature on this death.

He looked up at the pole again. "I'm gonna' take a look for myself," he said to no one in particular. They might never prove this was other than an accident. And to any normal way of determining such things, the physical testing in labs, the engineering reports, the weight of scientific evidence would prevail. They would in fact be technically correct—if that were all that moved in this world.

He walked over to the yellow-helmeted worker and introduced himself. "I'm Johnny Hammond, a private investigator working with the police department. I need to take a closer look up there."

The worker shook his head, pointing up the electrical pole to a transformer still dancing with blue electric currents. "Sorry, no can do. We're fresh out of body bags."

"Won't need one, thanks," Johnny countered. "How about the bucket, and keep it ten feet away?"

The worker nodded, "Twenty. It's your life, but my job. Take these." The worker handed him his insulating gloves and coat. "And unless you want to end up a baked ham, don't even think of touching anything."

Eddie was still writing on his notepad when he saw the Chilkat Corporation's black limousine pull into view, very slowly passing before the accident scene. The window rolled down, and the face of Jessica appeared.

Eddie looked over his shoulder to Johnny, who had now talked the utility worker out of his coat as well as his gloves and was just putting them on as he stepped into the lift bucket.

"Johnny!" he shouted.

Johnny looked back to see the limousine, and Jessica—she was surveying the scene with a detached calm. When she spotted Johnny, she stared back at him, even as she rolled up the window between them, and the limousine glided on its way.

Johnny threw off his gloves, leaped down from the lift bucket, and began running toward Eddie's parked police cruiser.

Eddie ran after him, shouting to the nearest policeman, "Check for explosive residue!"

The worker saw him leaving and shouted. "Hey! My coat."

Johnny and Eddie jumped in, Eddie taking the wheel.

"They won't find any, Eddie," Johnny pronounced. "Residue."

"What the Hell she doin' here?" Eddie said.

"'What the Hell' is right, Eddie," Johnny answered.

"She didn't even stop," Eddie said.

"Would you?" Johnny asked.

Eddie just shook his head slowly in consternation.

Nothing was adding up, but he knew Eddie would see her appearance in a different light than what he was now seeing, or feeling. But he was chasing a way into her world.

"Johnny, we should pick her up," Eddie said, speeding up the car to stay behind her.

"Not yet. I want to follow her," Johnny said. There was nothing he could explain to Eddie yet—he needed more time.

"Who do you think told her about the accident?" Eddie asked.

"I don't know," Johnny said, "But I'm going to find out."

"You mean ask her?" Eddie said.

"Explanations from her, Eddie...she's got 'em, they make sense, only they don't...the more you follow them, the more lost you get. I'd rather know where she's going."

"Ah, this lady, I'm thinkin' she's gotta be goin' bowlin'," Eddie said.

Eddie was right, Johnny thought. Normal logic just was not working here. He felt sorry for her, too. Losing two brothers like this would shake up anyone.

"She's scared, Eddie," he said.

"No. If you ask me, she knows more than she's saying," Eddie responded.

"Maybe, Eddie, or maybe she knows more than she knows," Johnny added.

"You wanna' put that in English?" Eddie looked over in his direction.

"I think you were right, Eddie, there is something in her, but I don't think you'll get it out of her by asking. It will have to come some other way."

"You mean, meet her at the bowlin' alley...so to speak..." Eddie said, twisting his mouth and raising his eyebrows.

Suddenly the limousine ahead sped up, disappearing under an overpass around a corner.

"Watch it!" Johnny said as he lost sight of the limousine.

Eddie floored the accelerator and they shot through the underpass, to another bend in the road, but the black limousine was gone.

Eddie surveyed the road. "There!" Eddie whipped down the first side street, a tree-lined suburban boulevard. High winds blew falling branches down upon the car as they drove.

Eddie said it first. "She's gone..." He stopped the car.

"Maybe not," Johnny said, looking up to the power lines overhead, swinging wildly in the wind.

Eddie looked up, following his gaze. A branch blew down on the windshield. Eddie slowed the car down.

Johnny tried to remove the branch by reaching through the window and around to the windshield but could not. Someone would have to get out. There was a loud buzz coming from the overhead transformer. He looked to Eddie, who responded with a grimace.

"I love you, Johnny, but ahh..."

For a moment neither of them moved or said a word.

"Right," Johnny said, then opened the door. He hesitated.

"My case," Eddie reminded him, "your investigation..."

"Right," Johnny said again. Then, with a sideways glance to Eddie, he stepped out.

Immediately, a ferocious gust of wind struck him, nearly knocking him off his feet. He took hold of the car door to secure himself and looked back up at the power lines. Another gust struck, and the power lines violently whipped side to side. Johnny threw the branch off and started to get back in the car when a thought hit him. He looked up and down the power lines to each horizon.

They were looking in the wrong place. The power lines were alive for miles, for hundreds of miles. It could be anywhere. No, not anywhere. Somewhere.

But he knew where to look. He knew how to look because he had been taught. Only he had forgotten—more than forgotten—he had turned away, turned from his own heritage, from three thousand years of ancient knowledge.

The wind roared and threatened, but now he stood his ground and drank in its power, planting his feet on the ground this terror walked. He would walk its path, find its dwelling place.

He got back into the car.

"What now?" Eddie asked.

"Mark Ames. We've got to make sure he's safe."

Eddie picked up the car radio. "I need two squad cars at the Mark Ames residence."

Johnny and Eddie headed across town to Queen Anne Hill. David was dead and now William. Johnny wondered if he should tell Eddie about the curse but decided against it.

The drive passed quickly. They pulled up in front of a ten-story condominium complex. "This the place?" Eddie asked with surprise.

"It's the right address," Johnny said.

"No accountin' for taste, huh?" Eddie said,

The complex was old and run down. There was no reason for a millionaire like Mark Ames to live there. Maybe they would find one.

On the top floor of the condominium building, Johnny and Eddie, flanked by two police detectives, walked down a long corridor.

"You want to break the news, or should I?" Eddie asked.

"I'll do it," Johnny said. He knocked.

A haggard thirty-year-old man came to the door, dressed in a velvet robe.

Johnny addressed him. "Hello, Mark."

Mark surveyed the situation, instantly distraught. "Johnny?"

"Mark, this is Lieutenant Eddie Landon."

Mark was looking at Johnny, not Eddie, "He's dead," Mark said.

Johnny said nothing.

"Billy's dead," Mark said, feeling it, not needing confirmation. "Isn't he?"

Johnny said, "I'm sorry—did your sister call you?"

Mark froze, answering mechanically, "No, no one called."

Johnny just looked at him, not sure what to make of his response, then said quietly, "Mark, I think you should let Lieutenant Landon take you into protective custody."

"No," Mark answered. "I will stay here."

"Stay here, then," Eddie said. "We'll just keep some men with you."

Mark spoke as if in a trance. "It won't stop."

"Mark," Johnny tried to reach him, but he was still lost in fear. "Mark, can you help us? Can you tell us anything? Do you know what's going on?"

"It won't stop," Mark repeated. "Raymond taught us."

"Mr. Ames, maybe you should sit down," Eddie said,

Mark hesitated. "He said once it began, it would not stop."

Your uncle, Raymond Ames?" Eddie asked, "Said it would not stop?"

But Johnny, anxious about Jesssica, persisted, "Mark, do you know where your sister is?"

Mark answered flatly, "Half-sister. They took her away when she was seven. I never knew why." Mark just shook his head, absorbed in his own thoughts. "I never knew why."

Johnny took hold of his arms. "Think. Both your lives could be in danger."

But Mark was drifting deeper into his own world.

"He doesn't know, Johnny," Eddie said. "We've sent two cars out to her place. We'll just have to wait."

Johnny was looking at Mark, trying to understand what had taken hold of him. Then he checked his watch. "Then let's hope she shows before morning." Johnny looked to the two detectives. "You don't open this door to anybody until after eleven thirty tomorrow morning.

"You've got it," one of the detectives responded. Johnny and Eddie went to the door. Johnny looked back to the three men. It did not feel right. Nothing felt right. But he walked out with Eddie and closed the door behind them.

Eddie looked at him. "Now who told him? What the Hell's goin' on here? You think Jessica called him?"

"As though he was expecting it," Johnny said, as they boarded the elevator.

"Like he had something to do with it?" Eddie asked.

"No, more like feeling an accident about to happen," Johnny said.

Johnny pressed the lobby button, and they began to descend.

"It's enough to give you the creeps," Eddie said. "And what's eleven thirty?"

Johnny's mind kept going back to the power lines. His instincts told him there was a way to get closer to the source of these killings. And he knew how he would do it.

"Johnny? You with me?" Eddie asked. The elevator doors opened, and Johnny stepped out, with Eddie right behind him. Johnny wanted Eddie to come, but he did not know if he had the right to ask him. "I've got an idea, Eddie," he said.

"What's eleven thirty, Johnny?" Eddie pressed him.

"I don't know yet, Eddie." Johnny answered.

"But you'll let me know when you figure it out, right?" Eddie said, not trusting that Johnny would.

"Sure," Johnny said, not meaning anything at all. He knew what he wanted to do, but not exactly why he was doing it. He knew he needed Eddie if he was going to get anywhere but couldn't even explain that to him. Even if he could, Eddie would not want to go with it. He had to do this one on the run.

Luckily, he saw a cab passing and flagged it down. He jumped, shouting to Eddie, "Meet me at the helicopter pad in thirty minutes!"

What the fuc— ?" Eddie shouted, but his words were cut off by the closing door.

What the fuck was right, Johnny thought. All he had was a gut feeling.

At least the police chief still owed him a favor.

Into the Mouth
of the Beast

When he arrived at the police station, Tommy Brubeck was waiting for him. Tommy was the best chopper pilot on the force.

"Chopper clear?" Johnny asked.

"Cleared and ready," Tommy answered.

"Then let's get up there. Lieutenant Landon's right behind us." They walked past the front desk toward the elevators. Johnny shouted to the desk sergeant, "Tell Lieutenant Landon we're on the roof!"

A minute later, he and Tommy were climbing into the chopper. Tommy started her up. The chop of the rotor filled the air, flashing the roof lights above like stroboscopes. Fierce winds buffeted them as he readied the chopper for lift off. Then he turned to Johnny.

"Where we going, Johnny?" Tommy finally asked.

"East," Johnny said.

Eddie came running and shouting up to the chopper, holding open the door. The noise of the rotor was deafening.

"What the Hell you think you're doing?" Eddie yelled.

"You almost missed us, Eddie, hop in!" Johnny yelled back.

"Who requisitioned this thing?!" Eddie asked, doubting any right answer.

Trust me," Johnny said.

'Right..." Eddie shot back. "Tommy?"

"Paperwork is clear," Tommy told Eddie.

"When pigs fly," Eddie sat, shaking his head, and climbing in. "You got something or not, Johnny?"

Johnny shouted, "The transmission lines! If there's a short upline, it'll be lit up like a Christmas tree!"

"A Christmas tree, huh? We'll be the ones lit up like a Christmas tree," Eddie shouted back. "And what the Hell good is finding some goddamn short!"

The truth of the matter was that Eddie liked adventuring with him, not that he would ever admit it.

The pilot lifted the chopper off the pad and headed into the night.

"Try not to get us killed." Eddie pleaded.

But Johnny finally knew what he was doing. He answered dead seriously, "I've got to feel it, Eddie. I've got feel it if I'm gonna' hunt it."

"Oh, Jesus," Eddie said.

Johnny was ready. He was going in, and he would come out, and when he did, he would have something. Maybe not much, but enough. "Hang on!" he yelled.

The helicopter climbed high above the city lights and turned toward the mountains. Soon they were following the power lines up the rugged slopes of the moonlit Cascade foothills.

"How far we gotta' go?" Eddie asked, not really expecting an answer.

The foothills fell away. They entered a mountain pass, skimming dangerously atop twelve transmission lines strung between a double row of twenty-story towers. High winds swayed the lines.

Johnny shouted over the sound of the rotor, while Eddie and tried to jot on his note pad and hold on to something at the same time, shouting to the pilot. "Easy, huh? I've got a pension coming and I don't want to waste it. Never made it the Bahamas."

Johnny spoke, to himself, to Eddie, to the night, to it, out there." The Tlingit warriors hunted their prey by three rules:"

Eddie continued his non-stop protest. "You're droppin', Tommy! Dammit! Is stayin' alive one of 'em?"

Tommy piped in, "Tlingit. Headhunters, right!?" going with the wild adventure.

Johnny continued, with a rhythm he knew instinctively. "One: to find him, let his heart beat in your chest!"

A blast of wind buffeted the chopper as the chopper dropped down into the gulch. The pilot desperately wrestled for control. Johnny sat perfectly still, his eyes fixed straight ahead, his resolution deepening. For one perilous moment, no one spoke as the chopper made its way over the rows and rows of high-power lines.

Johnny continued intoning, "Two: to stalk him, breathe when he breathes!"

A fiercer blast of wind swung the whole chopper wide of course. Johnny smiled, a deep ancient smile. Something was listening.

Another blast. Again, Tommy wrestled for control.

"Three: to kill him, show them your face to see theirs! Bring her lower, Tommy!"

Tommy hesitated.

"Now, under!" Johnny ordered.

"No, Johnny!" Eddie shouted.

"Under! Cut her under!!!" Johnny yelled.

Tommy dropped the helicopter down, under the huge towers of the power lines. The wind roared, tossing them from side to side.

Johnny leaned out, his face battered by the rain and the wind. Now he was the stalker. He shouted. "Bastard!" His anger was rising inside him, inside from a place deeper than he could fathom. Against the killer, against the murderer of his friend, against every terrible injustice he had ever seen or known. Against himself and his own transgressions. The wind slammed them off course. "Show me your face!" Johnny screamed into the night, against the wind.

Another huge gust of wind slammed into the chopper, jarring it half on its side, knocking Eddie into Johnny, but Tommy pulled her out level again.

"Coward!!!" Coward!!!" Johnny roared. "I'll find you! I'll kill you!" Another gust of wind buffeted the chopper. The motor faltered, then recovered. Eddie had turned white as a sheet. Tommy deftly executed an emergency maneuver, pitching into the roll, losing altitude rapidly. He flicked on the searchlights—the ground was coming up fast. "Hang on," he said, then expertly but harshly maneuvered the ship into a stable course and headed out of the valley.

Flashing bolts of lightning illuminated the chopper as Johnny pulled back his rain-soaked face, exultant.

His heart was beating so wildly in his chest he could feel his blood pounding through his entire body. The rise and fall of his breath was all that he held on to, the only ground to stand on...as he whispered, "I'm coming for you, you son-of-a-bitch."

On the ride back, Eddie would not talk to him.

Johnny had to take it. He could not explain. Barely to himself. But now he had gotten hold of something, and he did not want to let go. Through the landing, all during the drive home, he carried it with him in his belly and his chest.

Even in his bed, when he lay his head back on the pillow to sleep, it was there. Alive, inside him. Even possessing him in his dreams—he could not escape it. Now for the hunter possessed, sleep was not sleep, but a traveling in another world, a journey in search of a vision. And there were sounds of the night, of the wind...he was moving in and out of sleep, of dreams, of this world, and another...

Even when the morning sun pushed its warming rays into his bedroom, he was still flying strong on the mountain, tracking his preying running over the landscape below.

A Night for Two

...now a dark figure is approaching the foot of the bed. In candlelight. The figure is himself, his face, but much older. On the wall, above and behind his face, there is a wolf's head, with glowing red eyes. The dark figure draws closer.

"No!" Johnny awoke, jerking himself into a sitting position.

A real human figure, highlighted by a shaft of late morning light pouring through the closed curtains, stood at the foot of his bed. He whipped out a pistol from under his pillow, aiming it at the figure.

Jessica stood over him, waving a key. It was the second time he had pulled his gun on her.

"Lot of keys lying around this place...that breaking and entering?" she asked.

"You shouldn't be here," he said. It was the first thing that came to his mind.

"You want me to go?" She spoke gently.

"No." No, he did not want her to go. She had answers he wanted, whether she knew it or not.

"You were having a bad dream," she said, staring into his eyes. "I have bad dreams." She let her dress fall to the floor, "I can fix yours..." She stood naked, her chest rising and falling in long deep breaths, maintaining her gaze.

Johnny laid his gun down beside him on the bed, trying to recover his composure to offer her some condolence, hoping it were only her shock that was causing her strange behavior.

"Jessica, your brother, William..." but his thoughts collapsed before her approaching nakedness, his will dissolving. He could not withstand her spell.

She was moving toward him. "Half-brother. My father died when I was born," her words floating to him as she stepped nearer to the bed, and then climbed onto it, crawling to him on all fours. "I am sure they wanted to tell you they did not grow up with me...we don't have much time..." She ran her fingers over his chest, slowly lowering her lips toward his. "...on this earth..."

He should have found her words chilling, but he did not. He should have stopped her, but he was already moving with her. How could she be finding him when he could not find himself? Touching him when he had gone so long without touch.

His protest came from his mind, not his heart. "Jessica..." he said, not knowing what words would follow...

"I saw it in your eyes on the plaza...you want to fuck me, don't you?" she asked.

She used that word innocently, softly, as though knowing no other with which to make an offer of lovemaking.

"Put your clothes back on," he forced himself to say. It was a professional voice, the voice of reason and caution, but the sound of that voice was not registering now in her world, because now there was not even a thread between their two worlds to carry those words to her ears, and so he let those words go, like leaves on a stream.

She crawled over him, letting her breasts hang over him.

"No more investigation?" she asked quietly.

The investigation, what was he doing? He was following it. Following her. Following it through her. Or did he just want her? No, there was something more, something out there. So, he did not stop her.

Again, she lowered her lips next to his, barely kissed him, and whispered, "We're going to die, Johnny..."

He pushed her back, holding her shoulders, looking into her eyes.

She kissed him softly, once. "I don't want to die."

"No...," he said, feeling only the lingering sensation of those lips on his, and the warmth of her body next to his.

"Let me help you, Jessica," Johnny said. "Help me help you."

Jessica smiled, a distant smile, not hearing him, lifting the sheets to look down his belly. "But you are helping me."

She grazed her breasts over Johnny's chest, biting she bit the side of his neck, hard.

He gasped.

"You taste good," she continued, as though not hearing his outcry.

He touched his neck with his fingers, saw blood on his fingertips. He felt trapped, unable to move. He had to get control of this. Now.

She licked his finger. "I didn't know that before." She began lowering her kisses down his chest.

Summoning his will, he denied her. He pulled her gently back up, bringing her face to his, holding her gaze.

"You want me to go?" she asked. She was playing with him.

Her eyes remained open, staring, focused, as though seeing through him. He leaned aside, out of her line of sight. Her eyes were fixed on the digital clock. It read, 11:24 AM. The time of the next killing had passed, or was the phone about to ring?

He felt a sudden tenderness toward her, a protectiveness, and he saw a way out. He followed it. He said, "I'm not going to let anything happen to you." As though that might quiet his passion. It was a lie—he knew it. He did not have that power, and it opened a sudden emptiness in him, between them. He wanted more.

She only watched, as though reading his thoughts, to finally announce, "Then I'll stay." She cuddled up to him like a child.

He felt her close, felt her vulnerability, and just lay there, staring up at the ceiling.

"I wish I had known you before," she said softly, simply.

He didn't know why, but he wished it, too.

Through an Ancient Time

Eddie and Johnny stood on the rear upper deck of the Washington State ferry.

Johnny watched the morning skyline of Seattle recede into the distance, then turned toward their destination on the western shore, from the fading light of the Cascade mountains in the east to the glistening snow-capped peaks of the Olympics in the west.

Eddie turned with him, then lit a cigarette, taking a long drag.

Johnny snatched it from his hand, inhaled, and threw it overboard.

"Hey!" Eddie snapped.

"Thought you didn't like living dangerously," Johnny quipped.

Eddie lit another. "Thought we didn't fuck suspects."

The comment caught Johnny off guard. He did not know whether his indignation came on his behalf or hers. He just said, "Nobody's fuckin' anybody."

Eddie sucked on his cigarette. "Boy, you got a lot to learn..."

Johnny looked back to the receding skyline, not answering. There was nowhere to go with this conversation. How could he explain something he hardly understood himself? That he had slept beside her, and nothing had happened? That it was really part of the investigation? It sounded ridiculous even to him.

Eddie eyed him, exhaling far into the air. "Thin ice, partner, thin ice..."

Johnny changed the subject. "Prints back on that woman yet?"

Eddie let him. "Nothing. No passport, no entry record, no clothing labels, zip!"

"Anything else?" Johnny asked.

"Just this. Jessica is approved to see confidential corporate records. William and Mark aren't. David wasn't either. They're all her stepbrothers. Guess Austin Ames didn't like the first wife."

"But they were still running the corporation," Johnny said.

"Until she showed up. It's in the bylaws," Eddie said. "And some blind trust holding a major block of stock controlling the voting rights for what Jessica does not control."

"Bylaws," Johnny spit out, checking his watch "blind trusts..." But he was not thinking about the by-laws. He did not give a damn about the bylaws, "I feel like I'm hunting shadows," he said.

"Hers or yours?" Eddie asked.

"What time you got?" Johnny asked.

"Two-thirty...or maybe they're hunting you," Eddie said, in a way that made Johnny feel that, despite his hard line, Eddie was genuinely concerned about him. He added, "May be time to get out, Johnny."

Johnny could not tell him it was already too late. Last night he had crossed the line. Anyone else would have said nothing had happened, but everything had happened.

The investigation had become his grail against his better judgment and all instinct. Now he was holding on to it, to hold onto that piece of himself.

The ferry pulled into the dock. Johnny watched the crew throw and secure the ropes, then lower the chains that blocked the deck exits.

"Let's go, Eddie," he said, feeling glad that Eddie was there.

The shanty they were looking for was only a half mile from the ferry terminal, so they walked the distance.

The road led to an unmarked dirt trail which they followed down toward the shore. The trees quickly thinned, showing the shanty up ahead. The afternoon light was waning.

On the porch, facing down the shore, the old man Frank Johnson and his mother sat, quietly, staring across the sound.

Johnny stopped. "Why don't you hang back, Eddie? I think I'd better do this alone."

"Yeah, sure," Eddie said, deferring to Johnny's judgement.

As Johnny approached, the old woman gestured and said something to the man in her native tongue. The man looked solemnly to Johnny, then stood in greeting.

"Grandmother says, 'Welcome, shadow hunter.'"

Her words struck to the core of him, as though she had not bestowed the name, but revealed it. But he knew the name was not an honor, but a duty. Johnny nodded respectfully to both, but the woman launched into a spirited response of fear, anger, and appeal. He understood everything, understood too much. Her spirit reached him before her words.

The old man translated. "She says, she was never afraid to die. Now she hears the burial grounds will be stolen, and she fears her spirit will wander the earth forever."

She continued in her native tongue, waving toward the near hills.

The old man continued for her, "Already you have come to take away the earth, and the skulls of our ancestors roll down the hillsides."

Johnny nodded to the old woman and spoke to the man. "Tell her there is nothing I can do about that. Tell her—"

The old woman waved her hand in the air, as though understanding perfectly, and answered him strongly.

The old man translated again. "She says you must stop it or more will die." The old woman added more, snatching something invisible from the air, making a fist.

"You, too, will die, mixed blood, running before the Whites."

Johnny was immobilized by the old woman's stare. He felt in his blood the old poison of a shame he thought he had banished. He was one-half Blackfoot, but he never thought about it, never told anyone, never lived it.

The old man spoke for himself. "You will die like Joseph—inside." The old woman nodded wisely, as though seeing something in Johnny that he did not know himself.

Johnny pressed on. "Joseph? Who is Joseph?" he asked.

"Joseph Menchaca sold the land. Now his spirit wanders, even though his body remains, in Bellingham."

"Bellingham?" Johnny asked.

"He left his land. He left in the night. He left his people. To the hospital in Bellingham." The old man shook his head sadly, as though nothing could be more incomprehensible. "Then he broke his promise. He sold our grandmother's land." He pointed to the north.

"When did you last see him?" Johnny felt something, some thread to follow.

But the old man's face turned to stone.

The old woman waved some ritualistic gesture toward Johnny—he looked at her, suddenly realizing she would die soon. Johnny knew they would say no more about this man called Joseph.

"Tell her, the burial ground will not be disturbed. Tell her I give her my word."

The old woman nodded, as though not needing a translation, and spoke kindly. Johnny looked to the old man for the translation.

"She says she will pray for your life," the old man said solemnly.

Johnny felt the power of the blessing, knew he needed it. He met her eyes with the respect due an elder.

"Thank you...grandmother," Johnny said reverently. He turned slowly as the last sliver of sunlight slipped below the dark horizon, and the dusk deepened to show only dull shapes surrounding him.

He walked back to Eddie, who looked to him with an inquiring glance.

"Bellingham," Johnny simply said.

"Bellingham?" Eddie asked.

"A man named Joseph. He must have been the one that sold this land to the Chilkat Corporation."

"I hate driving in the dark," Eddie responded.

"Just let me go. I'll be back. Just meet me at three tomorrow at the Public Market, under the clock. I still want to check out something with the security chief down at the Chilkat Corporation."

They took the ferry back and split up at the dock. Johnny hopped a cab down to the Chilkat Tower and made his way to Erickson's office.

Erickson stood when Johnny entered.

"Mr. Hammond. I'm sorry. I didn't know who you were before."

Military, always back to the military, Johnny thought. The one thing he was respected for was the one thing he was trying to forget.

"Call me Johnny," he said.

Erickson extended his hand. "I was there in the last days of Saigon, too. Patrick Dolan told me. Green Berets, Silver star...it's an honor," Erickson said.

What did it matter now, Johnny figured? At least he would be getting some co-operation out of Erickson now. He would take whatever he could get.

"That was a long time ago," Johnny said.

"Said you were a damn good detective, too," Erickson said.

Not exactly a detective, Johnny thought, but it still only reminded him of the wasted years he was trying to put behind him. "That's what I'm doing here. You come up with anything yet?"

Erickson sat back down. "Not yet, but I'm working on it. We're running out the logbooks twelve months to verify identification and employment of everyone that's been in the building."

"There's one other thing been on my mind," Johnny said.

"Shoot," said Erickson.

"Where did this company start to get where it is today?" Johnny asked.

"That's no secret. It was built on land. Mary Ames' land, Austin Ames' second wife. Her father owned it all, left it to her." Erickson offered.

Johnny said, "It must have been more than that. Like what happened afterwards?"

"Diversification. Austin Ames. And had some help from some key people I heard— don't know who. Now we have thirty divisions, everything from manufacturing chemicals to engineering consulting for nuclear power plants," Erickson said.

"It's a long way from a piece of the earth to the insides of a nuclear power plant, don't you think?" Johnny asked.

"I read some things about how that happened when I was trying to get on with Chilkat. That was mostly Austin Ames's doing. It was rumored he had some kind of background in weapons research with the army. But I always believed there was someone else in the mix. Still, he's the one that really built up the business with the defense industry," Erickson said.

"But he was killed. Know anything about that?" Johnny asked.

"Sure, you mean the tanker explosion in the tunnel? It was in all the papers. It was real bad. They had to identify him by the dental work in a couple of teeth fragments," Erickson said. "A real mess."

"Do something for me, will you?" Johnny asked.

"Sure," Erickson responded.

Johnny pulled out an old business card from his wallet, crossed out the front and wrote his phone number on the back. "Find out who Austin Ames's dentist was—ask him if he remembers making that identification, if anything unusual happened around that time. Call me or Eddie down at the station if you come up with anything."

"You think this could go that far back?" Erickson asked.

"Just doing my homework," Johnny said. It was true. He liked to put everything on the table and look at everything at least once. Let it all stir together in his mind until some pattern became clear. He did not tell Erickson it was just his instincts that told him what to put on the table.

Erickson nodded in agreement. "I'll get right to work on it," Erickson said.

"Thanks," Johnny said. "I'll be looking for your call."

Johnny walked out of the building and checked his watch. He would have just enough time to catch some Chinese food before he was supposed to meet Eddie down at the market.

...Eddie picked him up under the clock and they drove north. On the drive up, Johnny wanted to tell Eddie about the curse, but somehow could not bring himself to do it. Maybe he just did not want any other thoughts or opinions to cloud his mind.

On the Borderline

Johnny and Eddie drove onto the grounds of the Bellingham State Mental Hospital. The buildings were gray block, oppressive, leaden.

"What time you got?" Johnny asked.

"Six," Eddie said. "This place gives me the creeps."

"Yeah, a hell of a place..." Johnny nodded upward toward the ominous looking buildings.

They approached the main desk, where a large stern-looking receptionist, bifocals perched on her nose, awaited them.

Johnny stepped forward. "We're here to see a Joseph Menchaca."

The receptionist looked up, eyeing them suspiciously. Then she got up and walked into the glass enclosed office behind her. She said a few words to the doctor sitting there, who looked out at Johnny, then rose and appeared from the office.

"I'm afraid Mr. Menchaca does not take visitors," the doctor announced.

"I'm Johnny Hammond. This is Eddie Landon with the Seattle Police Department."

"Has something happened?" the doctor asked.

"You might say that," Eddie said. "We can barely keep up with the body count."

"Joseph only came back yesterday—," the doctor blurted out defensively.

"What do you mean, came back? He escaped?" Johnny asked.

"No, he just came back," the doctor said, not sure whether he should say more.

"Spill it, doc," Eddie said, "Everything. I get cranky when I'm hungry. And I'm getting real hungry."

The doctor hesitated, and then said, "Well, Joseph committed himself, so he was always in control of that. He's been coming and going for twenty years. He started as an outpatient then, for two years, to '72. Then he came in on a trust set up for his own care—what's this all about?"

Johnny pursued his own questions. "A trust? What trust?"

"I'm sorry. We don't inquire into our patients' financial matters. Unless, of course, they can't pay their bills," the doctor said.

"Yeah, real humanitarian," Eddie piped in.

"How does he come and go?" Johnny asked.

"He is picked up by a black limousine at the front gate by his chauffeur. That's all I know." The doctor seemed to be growing more nervous. "I'm afraid I really can't be of much help to you."

"Just take us to him, Doc," Eddie said.

The doctor nodded. "Follow me."

He led the way down the corridor, with Johnny and Eddie following.

"Can you tell me anything about his...condition?" Johnny asked.

"That is, I'm afraid, privileged information–"

Eddie interrupted. "Right, doc. You wanna' court order, or you gonna' save us the grief?"

The doctor hesitated again, then spoke openly. "Well, if you're asking me if I think he is capable of violence, I would say absolutely not. We observed some mild manic depression in him, but the only incident, if you could even call it that, is the time he became upset when someone brought a camera into his room. Didn't want to have his picture taken—but who does in this place?"

The doctor deposited Eddie and Johnny at the bedside of Joseph, a still handsome but elderly Native American man. He was sitting silently on his bed, eyes downcast, the top of his head showing a bald crown, with long white hair hanging down covering the sides of his face, down to his shoulders.

"Hello, Joseph. I'm Johnny Hammond. This is Eddie Landon," Johnny said with due respect.

Joseph said nothing, not looking up. Eddie jotted on his notepad.

"I spoke with your cousins in Bremerton," Johnny said.

The old man began nodding his head. "You're not the first..." the old man answered. Johnny waited patiently for him to continue. "...others have come...they made me sell my land..."

"Who made you sell your land?" Johnny asked.

The old man shook his head slowly, as though in great remorse. "My cousin sent them..."

"Your cousin?" Johnny figured he might as well just follow along.

"My cousin, Jessica."

Now, after all this, back to Jessica! Cousin? What the Hell was this all about? Johnny looked to Eddie.

Eddie picked up the card at Joseph's bedside. It read:

"Joseph Menchaca." Eddie shrugged to Johnny.

He did not want to ask the question of Joesph. "Jessica Ames?"

Joseph nodded.

"She forgets us, who are her blood, by our grandmother. She forgets us forever," Joseph said.

Johnny's head was spinning. "She never told me."

"She wants to forget us forever," Joseph said.

"Why? Why does she want to forget you?" Johnny pressed, but Joseph did not answer. "She sent people to buy your land?"

Joseph suddenly picked up a medicine rattle on the bed beside him and shook it violently. He lifted his eyes to Johnny. No pupils showed in his white eyes.

"That shirt is not a good color on you," he said, and began laughing hysterically.

Johnny, stunned, waved his hand in front of Joseph's eyes. No movement, nothing. He was completely blind.

Johnny backed off, withdrawing as though suddenly in deadly danger. Those words.

Eddie was at a loss. "Johnny?"

Johnny did not speak.

"What is it, Johnny?"

Johnny checked his watch. "We better get back."

"Hey, hey, wait a minute," Eddie said.

Johnny started to leave, "I'll tell you on the way."

"Yeah, you're a regular encyclopedia, Johnny," Eddie said.

But Johnny did not tell him on the way. He just asked for a couple of more hours to think. It was a long quiet, drive, and Eddie leaned back in his seat and fell asleep.

The Gardener's Cottage

Johnny finally turned onto Jessica's street. He found himself driving down a tree-lined avenue bordered by meticulously manicured estates, many surrounded by high stone walls. He found her address laid in tile on the stone columns of her entrance gate. The night was clear, the sky black and sharp with stars. He could see the mansion sitting on acres of land atop a bluff that dropped to the Puget Sound.

Beside him, Eddie woke up as he pulled into the circular drive of Jessica's mansion, passing the two police cars stationed there.

Johnny and Eddie, still yawning, hopped out of the car, and walked toward the entrance, as four policemen emerged from the cars. The entire grounds and house were dark. Only the half moonlight showed the grounds had not been tended for many years.

"Johnny," Eddie said. "What's the deal here? A blind Indian man tells you he doesn't like your shirt and knows Jessica Ames' name. So what? Unless you've never had anybody shake a medicine rattle in your face before."

Johnny could not answer, not without pushing Jessica front and center into this investigation. Oh, she was involved, he just did not know how.

The two worlds of his investigation were colliding and intersecting. Above and below. He would no longer be able to keep them apart. But he could not bring Eddie all the way in. Not anybody. He just said, "No, never."

It was a rotten thing to do, and he knew as he said it that it would not fly.

Eddie was pissed. "That's it, Johnny. You've had your two days. I got to bring her downtown for questioning."

Johnny said, "And then we'll lose everything."

"Lose what?! We don't got shit now! Or do you mean, you'll lose—you'll lose, Johnny,"

"You're wrong, Eddie, you're just wrong," Johnny said.

"Right or wrong, Johnny, I got to do my job. That was our deal."

"She just lost two brothers and she could be next," Johnny said. "David Ames was a good friend, and you said you'd ride with me on this one, Eddie."

Eddie was exasperated. "I have been, Johnny, you know I have been," he said, starting to give in despite himself.

"Give me another day, Eddie. One more day." Johnny hated to do it to him, because Eddie was such a soft touch, but he needed every hour he could get.

"Damn it, I knew it. I knew it, and there goes my ass," Eddie said.

Johnny just took it as a yes.' "Thanks, Eddie. You won't—"

"Yeah, I know, I won't regret it," Eddie said.

Johnny anxiously knocked on the door. Nothing. He knocked harder.

"Jessica..."

He waited.

"Jessica!" he called louder through the door.

"She's in there..." one of the policemen said with certainty.

"This place looks like something out of the Munsters'," the other policeman scoffed.

With dead seriousness, Eddie added, "More like a morgue."

They were right. Everything was overgrown, falling down, left alone for twenty years. Johnny looked off to the right, where a small cottage stood alone, with broken windows and cobwebs, obviously uninhabited. It was overrun with weeds and shrubs, a high stone wall surrounding it, with a now rusty broken iron gate.

"What's that?" Johnny asked.

"Guest cottage?" Eddie guessed.

Johnny stared at it for a moment... "Or a gardener's."

Johnny walked over to it, through the gate, and around back. Strange. Against the back wall of the cottage was a flowerbed of fresh soil, weeded and tended. In the moonlight, he could see a row of three equally spaced carnations, and then two more that had been pulled up by their roots and laid back down in perfect order. Johnny knelt down on one knee on the grass and picked up one of the torn carnations.

The sound of a garage door opening broke the quiet of the night. Engine roaring, a black limousine whipped out and raced down the driveway.

Johnny ran back to his car, shouting, "Eddie!"

One of the police cars pulled out to follow the limousine. A police officer ran up to Johnny—it was Patrick.

"Johnny, Mark Ames wants to see you. He's scared, says he won't talk to anybody else."

Johnny, torn, watched the limousine and the police car disappear down the drive.

Patrick, seeing his concern, added, "We'll watch out for her, Johnny."

"Alright, Patrick. Thanks," Johnny said, turning to Eddie, "We'd better get over there fast." He looked at his watch. It was ten forty-five.

Eddie said, "We'll take a cruiser."

Traffic was light. Twenty minutes later they found themselves in the condominium of Mark Ames, listening to him. He paced nervously like a man with a death sentence, stopping only to crush a cigarette into an ashtray already overflowing with butts. A TV played news in the background.

"The fucker, dirty old bastard. Why should I pay for his sins?" Mark mumbled to himself loudly enough for all to hear. "Why?"

Eddie finally confronted him, "How about losing the riddles and telling it to us straight?!"

Mark turned suddenly and strangely silent, turning his back and looking out the window, clenching his fists. Then he began pacing again.

The voice of the television newscaster filled the silence: "The man who poured gasoline on his five-year-old son and lit him on fire is free after serving six years of a life sentence..."

Johnny checked his watch again. He kept thinking about Jessica. She could die next. He wished he was with her, and blamed Mark that he was not.

He stepped in front of Mark.

"You have to tell us, Mark. You have to tell us everything you know. Mark!"

Mark ignored him, attempting to walk around him.

Johnny grabbed him. "You have to tell us now, Mark." Still no answer from Mark. "You're gonna' die. Your sister's going to die. Your whole family's gonna' be wiped out."

Mark just shook his head slowly, staring off into the distance.

What the Hell? Johnny raised his voice. "Mark, you got some dark secret, it's going to be whole lot darker six feet under. You hearing me?!"

Mark suddenly pivoted to face him squarely, shouting, "Screw you! I don't have to tell you shit!!! Leave me the fuck alone!"

Johnny glared at him, shouting "Your brothers are dead! David was my best friend. You could be next, you—"

"What the Hell do you know about it?!" Mark yelled. "You don't give a damn about me! You're screwin' her, aren't you?!"

Johnny lunged for him, grabbing him.

Eddie jumped in to break them apart. "Johnny!"

Johnny lunged for him again.

"Johnny!" Eddie shouted, using all his strength to restrain him.

"Damn it," Johnny said, still glaring at Mark. "Fuck him, Eddie...let's get out of here."

Johnny turned and left. Mark was right. Jessica was the only one on his mind. Eddie said to the police officers. "Sit tight, guys. And call in anything suspicious, anything. We'll be back to you in the morning."

Eddie hurried down the corridor after Johnny. They reached the elevator together. Johnny pressed the call button and the doors opened.

Johnny looked into the eyes of each cop standing to either side, one after the other, cleared them in his mind, and stepped in. The elevator doors closed.

Eddie checked his watch. "It's eleven eighteen, Johnny."

He did not want to know that. He did not want to know what time it was ever again. Who would be next, Mark or her?

Now all he could think about was her safety, and the four minutes between now and a time when he might no longer hear her voice again or look into her eyes.

"Johnny?" Eddie asked when he did not answer.

Time was moving toward an end, seconds were passing. Silence approaching.

"Yeah," he said. Then he pressed the button, and they began to descend. He was sweating inside. Like a doomed man looking at the gallows, he pulled back his sleeve and looked at his watch. 11:19, its digital display read.

Johnny looked up to the overhead panel, watching the floors count down.

Eddie watched him with concern, knew he was thinking about Jessica.

Johnny continued staring up at the elevator floor display.

The elevator reached the ground floor. The doors opened. Johnny checked his watch again: 11:20. They stepped out of the elevator. They began walking down the hall toward the exit. Johnny felt each step tick off another second. He was counting his steps.

His legs grew heavy. He wanted to stop walking, as though it might stop time itself. They reached the front door of the building. He counted his last step. It was 11:21. He looked back toward the elevator, then to Eddie, and stepped out into the cool night air. He felt its freshness on his face and drew a breath as though it might be his last. Then they stepped down to the street and walked over to Eddie's police cruiser.

Eddie opened the door, reached in to pull out the radio. "...patch me through to 2 "L' 17..."

Instinctively, Johnny looked up, to the illuminated silhouette of the high-rise construction site opposite. There was a finality to the meeting of the steel girders, a horizontal and vertical precision that allowed no...no what? No music? No warmth?

"Where's she at now?" Eddie said.

A voice crackled back over the radio. "We lost her, Lieutenant."

"What?! Shit!" Eddie barked into the radio, "How the Hell do you lose a thirty-foot limo'?! She didn't go back to her place?"

Johnny looked to Eddie, his watch, the condo above, and his watch, the second hand sweeping toward ten...eleven...twelve.

A sound came like he had never heard before, and that he knew he would never hear again—a ninety-foot-long wall of glass, shattering into a million fragments, filled the air with a horrific chiming of glass shards crashing and erupting into clashing crystal fragments, chiming and chiming for long seconds that seemed to grow into minutes. He looked up to see the glass frag-ments exploding outward with no sound but that chiming, as time slowed...and a body flew out upon one of those gushers of glass, descending in a graceful arc two hundred feet through the air, to crash into the pavement.

Johnny and Eddie dove to the ground, covering their heads and necks with their arms, diving under the police cruiser on each side. Finally, the sound of the rushing explosion as glass shards fell to the ground all around them in a raining of glass, metal, and concrete. Then all was quiet. Time returned. Johnny turned his head—only a few feet away, the open eyes of the dead Mark Ames looked into his.

"Eddie!?...Eddie??!!" he called out.

"I'm okay," Eddie answered from the other side of the car.

Johnny instinctively reached over, taking the pulse in Mark's neck. Nothing. Johnny stood, looking down at the body, grotesquely twisted in death. And the only thing he could think of was that it was him and not her. She was still alive. Then he glanced up to the top of the condominium, and to the top of the new building under construction opposite. He rose and jumped into the car, shouting to Eddie. "Get in!"

They both jumped in, and Johnny started the car with a roar, whipping it around in a U-turn, and raced madly through a red-lighted intersection, swerving wildly between two cars.

He handed Eddie the car radio. "Call the team down!"

"Where we going, Johnny?" Eddie asked.

"Can you hear it? A heartbeat...we got a heartbeat," Johnny said, racing around another corner.

Eddie just looked at Johnny, knowing there was nothing he could say.

A Family Resemblance

Johnny pulled the car up to the sidewalk, screeching to a stop in front of his warehouse loft. He jumped out and raced in.

Johnny thrust his key into the door of his studio and rushed in.

He poured frantically through his stack of photographs, tossing them in all directions. He noticed he had a message on his machine and pressed the replay button to listen to his messages as he continued sorting...

"Johnny, it's Erickson. The name of the dentist who identified the dental remains of Austin Ames is William Collins. He had reported a break-in two days before. His records had been opened but nothing was taken. Call me if you need the contact."

He finally found the photograph he was looking for, the one of David standing before the studio window, taken the day before David's death.

He held the photograph with one hand as he picked up and dialed the phone with the other. He looked through his windows to the construction site opposite, the rising metal grid of another skyscraper. He knew the workers had been on strike for a month. He looked back down at the photograph, which showed the construction site...and there it was—the silhouette of a man, a helmeted construction worker walking the crossbeams. On the other end of the line, the phone was ringing.

"Come on..."

And continued ringing.

"Come on, Jessica," he said into the air. There had been a construction site opposite the Chilkat Tower as well. Both had been in line-of-sight.

Johnny stood with his back to the plate glass window, staring at the photograph, remote phone cradled between ear and shoulder. He waved the photograph slowly up and down in his hand. "Just breathe, you bastard, breathe...so I can hear you..." Behind him was the brightly illuminated steel grid-work of the rising skyscraper. He turned to see it, and his reflection in the glass. He looked down at the photo. He reached back into the pile of old photographs, finding one of David with his father Austin...then one of Austin with his wife Mary.

Then he saw it! Mary Ames looked eerily like a young Joseph Menchaca.

Suddenly, the huge electric engine of the crane atop the skyscraper started up. He put down the phone to look more closely. The arm of the crane began moving, whipped into full view, bearing a huge steel beam—the centrifugal force was pushing the beam farther and farther out—it was headed right toward him. Johnny dove for the floor at the far wall. The beam crashed through his front plate glass window, impaling his steel desk and office chair to finally lodge in the wall. A piece of the ceiling crashed down upon him.

Eddie crashed through the locked door, out of breath. "Jesus! Johnny! I saw it comin' at ya'!" Eddie lifted a large slab of sheetrock off Johnny.

"You okay?" Eddie asked.

Johnny threw another smaller piece of the wall off himself.

Eddie helped him up. "You all right?"

Johnny wiped the edge of his bloody lip, looked at the blood on his fingers, and said, "Sure, I just live for this shit. Come on!" He rushed out, with Eddie following him. He slammed open a door into a stairwell and bound down the flights, half running, half leaping to each landing until he emerged outside.

Two police cars pulled up, sirens running and lights flashing.

Johnny spotted an elevator cage descending on the construction site and ran toward it drawing his gun.

Eddie, pulling his gun, raced to keep up with him. "Over there!" Eddie yelled.

The police cars turned their spotlights on the sky-scraper. The elevator cage was descending. The policemen pulled their service revolvers as it reached the ground.

Johnny recklessly rushed forward and threw open the door, swung his aim into the cage—it was empty. The policemen advanced, shining their flashlights into the cage, but there was no one there.

The chop of a helicopter broke the night air above, searching the top floors with its search beams. Another car, a large white sedan, pulled up. A man emerged, waving his hands, "What the Hell's going on?"

A police officer responded. "Who are you?"

"Jack Evans. I'm the general contractor here."

Eddie kicked in, "Yeah, general contractor, huh? Well, we got Babe Ruth up there swinging your crane."

"That's impossible," Evans replied, "It's an electronically coded lock."

The policeman looked over to Johnny, then up to the top floors.

Johnny looked up, then to the contractor, "Radio controlled?"

"Computer," Evans said.

"We better watch it 'til morning," the policeman said.

Johnny glanced up. "Don't waste your time. Eddie, pull the computer control box. You can take it down to the down to the station."

Johnny started walking toward his car.

Eddie grabbed him, pulled him aside. "Where you goin', Johnny?"

"I got a date," Johnny said.

"Me, too. Let's go get the little lady," Eddie said.

"She's not involved, I'm telling you. She was not involved yesterday, and she's not involved today." Johnny stood his ground.

"Right, it's her shadow. So don't worry. I'll just bring her in and turn on the light. and nab the little son-of-a-bitch when he tries to run," Eddie said.

"What makes you think she's not next?" Johnny asked.

"It's a feeling I've got right here," Eddie said, holding up his little finger.

Johnny decided to change tact. "You owe me one, Eddie," he said.

"I'm all paid up!" Eddie said, "Letting you do your friggin' rain dance for the last forty-eight hours! You bring her downtown, or I will."

Eddie was serious this time. Johnny said the only thing he could. "Alright. Noon. At the station."

"Noon. Johnny, do it," Eddie said.

Johnny left. Time was running out. For the investigation, for him, for Jessica.

A Change of Worlds

Johnny pulled his car into the circular drive of Jessica's mansion. The police car stationed there flashed its lights. Johnny jumped out, looked around.

The entire grounds and house were super-illuminated with bluish green mercury floodlights, every room burning brightly like a sports stadium. He stepped to the front door, tried it. It was locked. He started to walk around the house when he remembered the flowerbed behind the cottage. He walked over to it. He looked down and remained staring for a long time. Now only two carnations were left standing, and two laying down. The fifth had disappeared.

He walked back to the main front door and kicked it open.

He could hear a stereo loudly playing in a far wing.

Johnny walked into a huge foyer, then a large circular ballroom, which was completely empty, with bare walls. He followed the music down a corridor.

The walls grew increasingly cluttered with mounted paintings and three dimensional mixed-art sculptures and paintings, seemingly all from the same artist. He stopped to read the signature: 'Jessica A.'

He continued. Passing a door on his left, he opened it. The room was dark and empty. He opened the door on the right—it led into an antechamber. Another door beyond, open a crack, revealed a lighted room...and he could hear dim conversation.

He walked into the anteroom, and peered in. He saw a man, naked, the chauffeur, standing in a pose.

Johnny looked around.

Then he heard Jessica's voice. "Hold...hold...if you move now, you're fired..."

Johnny swung around to see Jessica behind a sculptor's workbench, with an assortment of junk parts, fabrics, and wood, busily fabricating some fantastic indiscernible sculpture. She worked with intense concentration.

He found himself entering the room, looking cautiously around.

Jessica addressed him without looking up, "I'm working. Have a seat."

Johnny did not move, uncertain of this unfamiliar territory.

"I am trying to concentrate," she said with a tone of peevishness.

Johnny nodded, "Uh-huh..."

Jessica caught his non-believer tone and threw up her hands in exasperation. "Enough! Phillip, go."

Phillip exited and Jessica turned with fury upon Johnny. "Will you STOP haunting me?!!!" she shouted.

For a moment, neither of them said anything.

Then she steeled herself into a deadly calm razor's edge. "You should have a little more respect for the arts."

"Mark is dead, Jessica," Johnny said.

Jessica froze, then turned her back to him.

"There is no death," she said.

Johnny waited for her to say more.

She partially turned toward him. "Only change of worlds." Her eyes were filling with tears.

"For all your brothers," he said instinctively, watching for her response.

"Ten little Indians..." she said softly.

"Ten? What?" Johnny asked, stunned.

"Secrets and lies...my brothers are beyond sorrow now—that's what the Tibetan monks say," she said.

"I mean the ten little Indians..." Johnny said.

"It's not your fault, Johnny. You're out of your league," she said.

Where was she going with this one? "What league is that?" he asked.

Jessica turned back, picked up a ceramic vase, turning it on her fingers as she examined it.

"I need you to answer me, Jessica." Johnny said.

Jessica looked up, her patience with him exhausted.

"The answer, my dear Johnny, lies in your limited cranial capacity. Did you know that dolphins have larger brains than humans? I mean even accounting for weight, or the length of their spinal cords. That's how they measure it, you know. That's why, to you, everything simply is as it appears to be, or even worse, how you desire it to be."

Now Johnny had heard enough. Angry, he said, "So how is it really, Jessica?" He thought he saw some opening, but Jessica only glared at him. "You could die next! I'm trying to help you!"

"Help me? How? How, Johnny?" She brushed past him. "I know why you're here."

"What?" Johnny grabbed her. "Stop!" But maybe he was so angry because she was right.

When he touched her, she froze, dropping the porcelain vase she was carrying. Then she turned on him in a rage.

"You're a joke! An irritating little joke! What do you want?" Jessica sneered, and then turned and pushed through a set of double glass doors to stride out onto the lawn.

Johnny shook his head in confusion and disbelief. "I'm trying to keep you alive!" he shouted, watching her through the partially opened glass doors as she drifted out toward the far edge of a sea of tall grass.

She strolled out along a low stone fence, as if completely undisturbed, enjoying the soft breezes in the full moon. At the farthest point, near a low stone wall, she stopped, and seemed to be swaying slowly forward and back in some sort of reverie. He could hear the ocean waves crashing below beyond the bluff.

As Johnny stood on the other side of those glass doors watching her, he knew without doubt this would be his last chance to find her, to reach through her to whatever mystery lay beyond. He stepped out, through his own point of no return, even as he heard Eddie calling his name. He still believed he could make her trust him.

He pushed open the glass doors and walked out into the dense hanging air of night. The grass was thick and soft. He began walking, but it was not him walking. His legs were moving by some other will, maybe hers, maybe the will of that thing which he hunted... or was now hunting him.

He walked to her side. The bluff rode high over the Puget sound, edged by only a low stone wall. The surf was visible far below. The scent of blossoms filled the air...the scent of spring, in the autumn. A warm refreshing breeze blew up from the sound, around him, through him.

Jessica stood before the stone wall, looking out over the water. Her profile shined in the moonlight. She received him graciously, naturally, speaking first, "We're standing on an overhang. It's two hundred feet straight down," she said.

Johnny looked around and then stepped to the edge, looking down to the moonlit water lapping the shore far below, then down at the ground at his feet. He scraped at the gravel with the edge of his shoe, then looked at the striking profile of her face in the soft silver light.

"This reinforced?" he asked, cautiously avoiding inflaming her again.

"Steel and concrete..." She took a deep breath of the spring night air. "We're engineers. I love the air here..." she said, and turned to look over her shoulder, gesturing with her eyes. "My bedroom..."

Johnny looked back to the house, to a large iron-framed bay window on the second story.

"Sometimes I just throw open those windows and lie naked on my bed…" She paused, as though luxuriating in the sweetness of the night air through her skin. "This wind is warm, from the earth. But sometimes it's cool and electric, from the stars. I like to feel it on my nipples…"

Jessica noticed Johnny's expression. "Sometimes, alone, I can even come." She was courting some reaction, but he only listened.

"Your whole family lived here?" he asked.

Jessica laughed, immediately seeing through his pathetic attempt to gather information. "I suppose you can't help it. We all live in our own worlds, don't we? Ever been married, Johnny?"

"Once," he answered, not knowing why.

"Were you in love?" she asked.

Johnny decided not to answer, preserving his privacy.

Jessica continued as if in her own world, "…I always told myself, I'd rather die than stop growing…rather die than lose my innocence."

"Jessica, it's not going to stop," Johnny said forcefully. "You need to—"

She turned toward him, interrupting, scoffing, "But you're going to stop it? Such a little boy dream." She half turned away, falling again into her musing. "You know how you think you're living, but you're really not, because you're not feeling anything, and you're not believing anything, you're just going through the motions, while the real questions are passing you by?" She paused for reflection. "...after it kills me, it will stop."

Johnny was struck silent by her statement, for the first time really believing she might die, and he might not be able to do anything about it.

Jessica pointed overhead. "Sagittarius...see the three stars together? That's the belt of Orion..."

She turned toward him, reaching out toward his face, but then dropped her hand back to her side. Their eyes met.

How far he could travel with her...but he buried his feelings, steeling himself to continue. He said gently, "Jessica, I spoke with your cousin Joseph, today."

Jessica turned her back, looked up again as though not hearing him.

"...sometimes I feel like that's where I really belong, where I really am... like I was just left here with the smallest thread..." She gestured from her heart, as though tracing with thumb and forefinger a thread leading out to the stars. "...connected to my body here on earth..."

He looked at her, and said simply but kindly, "This isn't a dream, Jessica..."

A flash of heat lightning illuminated the estate.

Jessica looked around and up into the sky, as if listening for some message and then looked deeply into his eyes. "Yes, it is. Dreams are what make us, Johnny...maybe I've just had too many...But if you're looking for the place where your pain ends and mine begins..." Jessica smiled, and slowly, gently, took Johnny's fingers in hers. "...you'll never find it."

Her words struck home. Still looking into his eyes, she began kissing his fingers.

He felt it, could not control it. He was crossing the point of no return with her.

"Because you can never really touch someone until you feel the depth of their aloneness." She stepped closer to him. He could feel the heat of her body. "You should forgive yourself, Johnny....David told me about Lara."

Now he could not turn away. She ever so slowly caressed the side of his face.

"Home doesn't have to be so far away," she half-whispered, falling into his arms, into a long embrace...in the stillness of the night. Only the sound of swishing pine branches rose above the evening quiet. The half-moon was rising higher.

Later, in the drawing room, two empty wine bottles and two empty glasses stood before the fireplace. Johnny and Jessica sat on the floor on furs before the strong flames, Johnny leaning back, enfolding her in his arms and legs. Jessica held a book before them, reading aloud, while a movie played on the wall.

The film narrator spoke "And when the last Red Man shall have perished from the earth, and the memory of my tribe shall have become a myth among the White Man, these shores will swarm with the invisible dead of my tribe..."

On the home movie screen was the eerie image of a 1906 Edward S. Curtis film:

A forty-foot wooden war canoe, paddled by twenty Tlingit warriors in full war dress, approaches from a hundred feet out from shore. On its bow, with perfect balance, a medicine man, with a wooden head in the form of a giant beaked bird, and huge winged feathered arms dances a wild ritualistic dance invoking terror and victory.

Jessica continued, speaking over the narrator. "And at night when the streets of your cities and villages are silent and you think them deserted, they will throng with the returning hosts that once filled, and still love, this beautiful land...let him be just and deal fairly with my people, for the dead are not powerless...Dead I say?

There is no death, only change of worlds." Jessica looked up to the empty screen.

"It'll play again—I had it looped."

On the screen, the war canoe again approached the shore, a medicine man with a giant wooden eagle head atop his shoulders as his body dancing wildly on the bow.

Jessica was genuinely enthused. "See? You will never see this. It's gone from the earth, when the last medicine men died over the past decade. It's not a re-enactment—it's an invocation—his mind and spirit and blood fills with what he calls down from above."

Her warmth made him feel at home on the earth, as he had never felt before.

The film went black for a moment.

"My brothers could never understand that..." She pointed to the screen.

"This is all they want..." The screen now showed massive bulldozers and cranes leveling once pristine wooded shoreline..."

"And what's left, well, what's left, Johnny, is what we might find in each other, if we can find it..."

She stepped around to sit in front of him, touched her own heart and then his. "Then it will make us remember. It will make us feel." She swiveled back around, pushing her back into him, taking his arms and putting them around her. "I like being in your arms. They're different, like you, wild, angry…"

She fell back upon him, his arms enfolding her, her back to his chest. She let her arms fall open like wings and laughed a small laugh.

"Johnny…could you ever love me?" she asked.

He knew he could, and did, somewhere. It was a love that could only ever live in another world, not in this one. But he could not tell her that. Or tell her, at that moment, he could not imagine a life without her. Even if he had never met her, even if their paths had never crossed, it would be the same, because he had always felt her—was it her—inside of himself.

She smiled to herself, letting the question pass without an answer.

"Can you feel my heart beating? Like it's in your own chest?" she asked.

Johnny froze. A cold hand clawed at his heart. Why?

"Can you?" she repeated softly.

Johnny did not answer.

"Don't answer…Raymond would be jealous," Jessica said.

Something was wrong.

Jessica turned over on top of him.

"What?" Johnny asked. But his head was beginning to spin inside.

He gently extricated himself and sat up as though from a dream. He looked at a clock. Strangely, his vision was blurred. He blinked his eyes, growing very tired, and looked around the room anxiously. He reached for the wine bottle, studying it, wondering if he had been drugged.

Jessica smiled at him. "More? There's still one bottle left. I brought three up from the wine cellar for us."

Johnny looked at her as his eyes grew heavier, her beautiful face dimming. He did not expect to wake up.

◇   ◇   ◇

Johnny awoke groggy. It was morning. Jessica was gone.

"Jessica?" He stood, looked around, and stumbled to the corridor. "Jessica?"

Johnny emerged from the front door.

Patrick left his car and walked up to Johnny, glancing at his rumpled clothes with that big Irish grin.

"Everything okay in there, Johnny?" Patrick asked.

Johnny leaned toward Patrick, steadying himself by placing a hand on his shoulder. "Where is she, Patrick?" Johnny asked.

"We thought she was with you. Her car is still in the garage—we'll search the grounds," Patrick said.

Johnny looked around. "Forget it..."

Maybe his half-dazed state put him more in touch with her, but he knew, he could feel, she was not there. He also knew he would find her.

He found himself driving. His mind was empty except for a sense of her absence. He was not sure where or how he would find her. He just observed everything and everybody on the streets as he drove, letting all that he saw fill his mind like a river rushing by.

And for the first time, he saw those streets, with their morning life. He saw the children playing, and the dogs racing, the delivery trucks with their crates and hand-trucks, and the pedestrians, each with certain purpose. And him in his own world...pursuing what?

He turned off down a side street, followed it until it curved its way to another thoroughfare, which ran alongside a double set of railroad tracks.

He drove on, letting the miles pass around him. Finally, he spotted a solitary woman standing at a train stop, a scarf over her head. From behind, she looked like Jessica.

The train pulled in, blocking his view.

He whipped his car over and parked, leaping out to run around the end of the train. He jumped in through the doors as they closed on his heels.

An attractive young woman, amused with his energetic entrance, smiled to him. Johnny nodded to her, and then looked around. He walked through the car, looking at faces, searching for the woman with the scarf, but he could not find her, or Jessica.

He noticed a dazed, exhausted mother standing near the doors, holding her two-year-old daughter. A man leaned over to tease the little girl's ear with his finger, and she began to laugh. He thought he saw a perverse leer in the man's game, even as the face of the child grew radiant.

The train entered a tunnel. For a moment, the car lights blinked on and off, leaving seconds of darkness. He heard a voice beside him, a low desperate whisper. "I am the one you must love," he thought he heard. And then a short gurgling scream! Followed by the sound of a crumpling body. The train began to slow. The woman was screaming, He heard the sound of the train door opening and closing. The train emerged into the light—the child's mother, her face covered with sprayed blood, was still screaming. Johnny saw the man on the floor—it was the man who had been teasing the child. His throat had been cut from ear to ear. More screams filled the train car.

Johnny puts his fingers to his cheek, felt the blood where he had been nicked by a razor. The train pulled into an underground stop, and the doors opened. The crowd stampeded out in a panic.

Johnny rushed out, pushing through the crowd, searching frantically.

He ran up to a short man with long silver hair, and sunglasses, who was scrambling away. He caught up to him, ripped his sunglasses off—his eyes were all white—he was blind. The man smiled a toothless grin. What the Hell was this?

Johnny looked back to the tracks, running back to jump down into the track well, following the tracks back into the tunnel, racing into the semi-darkness. Another train came barreling around the corner. He leaped to one side and pressed his back up against the wall, grimacing as the train rushed by only inches from his face. The last cars of the train shot by. He looked up and down the tracks. Nothing. Just his breathing and the fading sound of the train rolling down the tracks.

◇　　◇　　◇

In the Chilkat tower, confused and disoriented, Johnny rode the elevator to Jessica's floor. The elevator doors opened.

He burst into Jessica's office, blowing by Jessica's receptionist, Jamie.

"Can I help you, Mr. Hammond?" Jamie asked, jumping up out of her seat to intercept him.

Johnny ignored her and entered Jessica's office. She was not there. He rushed back out to find Jamie on the phone, calling security. He grabbed the phone from her ear. She looked up startled, scared. There was blood still on Johnny's face and hand.

Johnny shouted, "Where is she?!"

Terrified, Jamie shook her head.

"Has she been here?!" he demanded.

She shook her head again, scared.

Johnny stormed out, headed downtown.

He burst into the police office, and strode to Eddie's desk, cutting through a wake of startled workers.

Eddie stood, spotting the blood seeping through the handkerchief Johnny held to his face.

"Johnny!" was all Eddie could say.

"Just a nick." Johnny wiped his cheek, looked at the blood on his fingers.

"I heard a voice on the train," Johnny said.

"I'll tell you what you heard," Eddie said. "It was Jessica Ames. We followed her to the train—we saw her get on! You shit on your deadline, Johnny. Now we got a corpse on that train."

"I was on that car, and she wasn't on it!" Johnny said.

"Bullshit!" Eddie challenged.

"She wasn't there!" Johnny repeated. "She wasn't there, Eddie!"

"You know what, Johnny, I really don't give a damn. All's I know is wherever she goes, people turn up dead. I'm bringing her in."

Then let me bring her in," Johnny said.

Eddie shook his head. "How come every time you decide to let it hit the fan, I'm standing in front of it? This investigation's over for you! Go take a cold shower and get this psycho bitch out of your mind! And what-ever else she is...I'm putting out the APB!"

"You owe me, Eddie," Johnny said with steel in his voice.

Eddie leaped up, grabbing him. "I'm done owin' ya', Johnny. I paid you. You used up all your credit. Now open your eyes!... Who the hell you workin' for? The fuckin' undertakers?"

"She couldn't have done it!" Johnny said.

Eddie held up three fingers. "How many fingers, Johnny?"

Johnny pushed his hand away.

Eddie kept pushing. "You drunk, Johnny? Your eyes goin' on ya'? Or just doin' your thinkin' below the belt?"

Johnny just looked at him, not saying a word, waiting for him to cool down. Then he said, "It's not how it looks."

Eddie looked at him incredulously. "How it looks? How it looks, Johnny?!!

You just spent the night with the only name on your suspect list! For Chrissakes—"

"She gotta' die before you take her off yours?!" Johnny shot back.

Eddie shook his head. "Jesus, Johnny..." There was a note of genuine concern in his voice. "She's givin' you the royal mindfuck. You probably already got her goddamn picture on the wall in your little fantasy land. Why can't you see what she is?" Eddie reached for the phone, "Just go clean up and think about it."

Johnny grabbed his wrist, holding the phone away from his ear.

"How do you see it, Eddie?"

Eddie pulled his arm away, picked up and threw down a manilla folder. "The sole survivor clause, Johnny! She read it! She owns it all now—everything–a bil-lion dollars' worth. Motive enough?!"

Johnny came right back at him. "Motive, bullshit. It's comin' at her, not from her. Look at the facts!"

Eddie shook his head. "Facts? You want facts!? In 1970 her mother, who was the original owner of all the land, was murdered when Jessica was six. 1971: Her fa-ther becomes the only suspect when the D.A. finds out she was divorcing him. A week later he's killed driving behind a tanker that explodes in a tunnel."

"Who owned the tanker?" Johnny asked.

"Who gives a shit? The indictment was coming down the next day—he was going to get the needle. But before he dies, he has the sole survivor clause written into the corporate bylaws. Now Jessica owns the corpo-ration by her father, and the remaining land by her mother. One neat package. End of story."

Johnny nodded as though seeing Eddie's great reve-lation "Well, there it is...greed, the oldest motive in the book."

"You got that right," Eddie said.

"Right...." Johnny said, "She's the sole survivor."

"She's the sole survivor," Eddie said.

"No. She's not the sole survivor! It's the corpora-tion! The corporation is the sole survivor, with a blind trust controlling it," Johnny said, and decided to take

Eddie's argument apart piece by piece. "What did Austin Ames do before he started the company?"

Eddie could not answer.

"Army weapons research." Johnny was winging it, based on what Erickson had told him. So, who owned the tanker?" Johnny pressed.

Eddie admitted, "We don't know who owned the tanker."

"The corporation. How'd they I.D. the body?"

"Are you losin' it, Johnny? Cause you're not making any sense." Eddie said.

"Dental records on two teeth fragments," Johnny said.

"Except the dentist reported a break-in the week before. Dental records were the only thing missing. Who the hell died behind that tanker?! We don't know. And Joseph Menchaca? Who the hell is he?! He disappears from Bremerton at the same time as Austin Ames' supposed death, shows up two days later at a psychiatric hospital with some Indian land in a trust for his health care. Who set up the trust? Put the money in it? Where did he get the land?"

Eddie, confronted by Johnny, had no answers.

Johnny hammered him. "What is this, Dunkin Donuts? I don't hear any gears turning up here," he said, pointing to Eddie's temple.

"So, he made a deal, so what," Eddie said, pissed, pushing his hand away.

"Not the point, Eddie. Not a deal! He would never sell the shoreline. But he would want to control it invisibly, through the corporation, through a sole survivor, or through a blind trust. Don't you see? Two plus two is not making four here! She's our only doorway in, and our only doorway out of this nightmare. You pick her up now, and we may just never wake up from it."

Eddie was silent for a moment. Johnny wiped his bloody cheek with the palm of his hand.

"And the train, Johnny?" Eddie asked.

"I don't know, Eddie. But she couldn't have done it. What's the motive? You don't have one. David and William—you got a blown-out window and a downed power line. Mark—who the Hell knows what that was. So, where's the evidence? We're still on the same case here. Don't forget that. You think I'd want to leave her on the streets if I thought she might kill somebody?!"

Eddie just looked at him, shaking his head, saying nothing,

Johnny said, "I'm gonna' go clean up." He turned and walked into the bathroom.

Johnny looked at himself in the mirror. Time was running out on him. He began washing his hands and face, leaning over the basin, trying to calm himself while his mind raced. Until now, he had been certain she had not been directly involved with the killings. That's what he had just told Eddie. The face of the dead man on the train came back to him. Could he have prevented it? He only knew he did not want anyone else to die. And if it was at Jessica's hands...no, he had followed out that line of thought and rejected it...he had to stay on the same course. If he left her trail, he had nothing.

He turned the faucet off. He looked up at himself in the mirror—and stopped. He turned the faucet back on, listened to the sound of the running water. He turned it off. Turned it on. Turned it off again. After his meeting with Jessica in her office, she had gone behind a door, and turned on a water faucet like this one.

Johnny emerged from the bathroom, prepared to continue the argument—with what he did not know. He had said everything he could.

But Eddie just shook his head, half in resignation and half in respect, offering, "You're gonna' need a few stitches for that, Tonto."

Johnny looked at him, the question in his eyes. He still didn't know if Eddie was going to let him keep control of the investigation.

Eddie gave him the answer. "I could lose my job on this one, Johnny, I let a murder suspect stay out. We'll have to put a watch her. And just until midnight. No more. Got it?"

"Thanks, Eddie," Johnny said. "I'm going back to the Chilkat Tower."

"Nice night for a drive," Eddie said, grabbing his hat. Johnny smiled.

They drove together to the Chilkat Tower Plaza, not saying a word. That was okay with Johnny. He appreciated the quiet. Maybe he just needed to go back to where it all began to get his bearings. Everything he had ever learned about human nature told him Jessica was not capable of killing, but the evidence was building against her, and the tension within him was becoming unbearable.

The plaza was empty. It was the weekend. Johnny stood again on the spot David died. He looked upward to the top floor, then across to the opposing lot, where the frame of the new skyscraper stood. He walked with Eddie to the main entrance, and they entered.

On the seventeenth floor of the Chilkat skyscraper, Johnny approached the empty window space. Only the yellow police tape stretched across it stood between him and the seventeen-floor drop on the other side. He stood on the edge, gripping the frame with one hand to secure his balance. A freezing wind was blowing on his face. He looked out to the night lights of the city.

He heard a voice directly behind him.

"Is it true the criminal always returns to the scene of the crime?"

It was her. He froze, realizing she could easily take them both through the window.

"An innocent person died today," he said, his back still to Jessica.

She stepped closer.

"Innocent?" She reached for his hand, removing it from the frame.

He did not know why he let her.

"How do you know?" she asked.

She moved closer, so he could feel her breath on his neck.

"You always know where I am," he said, ignoring her question.

"You always go where I'm going, Johnny."

She began breathing in rhythm with him. He noticed it. Her chest filled when his did. She exhaled when he did...at first subtly, then more audibly.

He looked down into the chasm below, helpless, knowing one push from her would end his life.

"I like breathing with you..." she said.

She was taunting him, feeding him back his own thoughts, hunting him.

He turned, trying to keep his mind from spinning.

He took her hands in his, turning them over to examine them. He saw nothing and felt suddenly exposed. He looked into her eyes, hoping to cover his real purpose. "...the hands of an artist..."

She looked into his eyes, held his gaze... She was reaching into his mind. She turned her hands over and back for him.

"Looking for blood? Gun residue? Explosive trace?" She smiled, eyes filled with light... "And I could have washed them," she added matter-of-factly.

Jessica surveyed the window frame and continued, "Architects should architect, and builders should build. But now it is profits above all, above quality, pride, integrity, above any human value. Capitalism is a beast we created to serve us——now we serve it. Monstrous, don't you think?"

Johnny felt half in one world, and half in another, as he edged away from the open window frame. He kept his eyes on the window edge, making sure he was not between her and the open space.

He did not know what else to say. He said, "I want you to live, Jessica."

She slowly lifted her forefinger to his lips..." Shhh..."

"I want you to live," he repeated, not sure why he said it again.

"And I want you to live." She said it as though the power of that bestowal was hers to grant, but not completely.

She smiled, then casually changed the subject. "Come to my office later?"

"Why?" He tried to say it naturally but was not sure if it was the right question.

"To take me home," she answered simply. "These things should not stand between us."

It was a delicate dance. "No," he said. "They shouldn't."

"Eight thirty," she said. "Be there or be square." She smiled, amused with herself, and the trite expression.

"I'll be there," he answered, not knowing whether he was pursuing an investigation or willingly joining her in some death pact. It didn't seem to matter. He only wanted to break through the wall of glass standing between them.

She turned and left.

A figure stepped out of the shadows, gun drawn. It was Eddie. He looked after Jessica. "That's some invitation."

Johnny looked down at Eddie's gun.

Eddie explained, "I'm pretty sure you can't fly, partner."

Johnny stared after her. "One I wouldn't miss for the world."

"Something strange came up," Eddie said, glancing at this notepad. "About Raymond Ames..."

"Her uncle," Johnny answered.

"That's the thing. He was her uncle, but not by Austin Ames, He was Mary Ames's brother."

"Not Austin's? He took the Ames family name?" Johnny asked.

"That's not all," Eddie continued, "he came out of the Special Forces, too, an explosives expert. Then got a Ph.D. in chemistry from Stanford. Raised Austin's family for seven years after he died, and then just disappeared. No one's heard from him since."

"Jessica said Raymond would be jealous.," Johnny replied, thinking aloud. "Who the Hell is he?"

"Jesus. This is some deep shit, Johnny. Watch yourself," Eddie warned.

"Yeah..." Johnny intoned.

Eddie frowned, noticing how strange Johnny sounded. "You okay? Still here on earth with us?"

Johnny gave no answer.

"Need a piece?" Eddie asked.

Johnny shook his head.

"Try to get that information back on Austin Ames' will. See if Raymond Ames is in there. I'll see you back at the plaza," Johnny answered.

"You didn't answer my question, partner," Eddie said.

"Still on earth," Johnny answered.

"Right. You know I got eyes in my head, don't you? Twenty years I've been' goin' with you, Johnny. You go into these women, and you don't come out, until somethin' drags you out, bloody and unconscious, screamin' for a little piece of your soul back. Only this time you're not gonna' come out, and I think you know that. And killin' yourself isn't going to make you who you were before 'Nam—before Phoenix. You can only do that if you stay alive."

Eddie began to walk away, then turned back to say, "Get it right, this time, Johnny." He left.

Johnny was left alone with Eddie's words. He knew Eddie was right. He could only think to go to the one place he had not gone. For a long time, the roads had been waiting to bring him there. Now all roads led there.

He drove, putting everything out of his mind. He was just driving. Until he was not. The car sat before the giant stone gates of a locked cemetery.

He got out of his car and checked his gun. An empty gesture, he knew. There would be no protection against the shadows he hunted here. He walked around to one side of the gate and jumped over the low wall.

On the cemetery paths there was enough moonlight shifting through the low clouds to see his way. He began walking down the gravel path, listening, peering out of the sides of his eyes. He heard a sound—and stopped. The wind was brushing the branches, one against the other.

He heard quiet steps—raccoon he thought. He continued walking, noting the gravestones, an obelisk, a cross, a mausoleum. He had fixed the directions in his head a long time ago. He had always known he would come here someday.

He turned down a side path, approaching a gravestone. It read: Chief George Hammond 1929-1988.

Johnny looked around, to be sure he would not be disturbed. He walked to the gravestone, and sat down, leaning his back against it. He heard the wind in the branches, and in the distance...the buzz of an electrical utility pole. He picked up a handful of soil, let it pour through his fingers, as sifted through her words in his thoughts.

"Ten..." He picked up another handful of soil. "...little..." ...poured it through his fingers. "...Indians." Jessica said it. Agatha Christie, 1939. A story of ten people on an island being killed off one by one, each one already implicated in a murder. The killings were not going to stop. But then who had David, William, and Mark killed?

Suddenly he looked up, feeling some presence.... When he was young, he had left his Native American father, turned his back on the old ways. During his lifetime they had spoken little. Only after he was gone had Johnny looked for him, tried with his heart and mind to reach through that impenetrable wall, to make his peace with his father. But his voice had traveled only half the distance, into that infinite wasteland between the worlds of the living and the dead.

He quieted himself, listening again to the wind in the trees.

He looked back down at the ground. He listened for a moment, then let his head fall back against the stone...closing his eyes, drifting into a waking dream.

For a long moment, there was only darkness, until the dream came...

A torch-lit tunnel...a barefoot six-year-old girl dressed in a nightgown. She was holding someone's hand, being led

through a dimly lit underground dirt tunnel. There was ter-
ror in her eyes...

The sound of a branch snapping woke Johnny from his dream. He lifted the gun before him. Again, the sound came. From behind, the shadow of a human figure passed over him.

Johnny whipped around and leapt to his feet, aiming the gun into the night. There was nothing there. The stillness of the night held him in a vise-like grip. But now he heard something. What was it? Where was it coming from?

In his mind?

Somewhere, he could barely hear a young girl crying, slowly fading away into the night breezes...

◇   ◇   ◇

Johnny pulled his car up to the Chilkat Plaza and began walking to the main entrance.

Eddie, who had been waiting, hurried across the deserted plaza to meet him, putting a hand on his arm, asking, "You going in?"

"She okay in there?" Johnny asked,

"Busy as a beaver, I'm sure," Eddie kicked in.

"What time she get in?" Johnny asked.

Eddie nodded. "Just before eleven. I would have given you three to one she was a no-show."

"Must be my lucky day. It always was a bitch to be stood up," Johnny answered.

Eddie looked him straight in the eye "No heroics, right? And no bullshit. By the book." Eddie glanced toward the road. "There's Patrick."

Patrick pulled up in police cruiser and hooped out.

Eddie repeated himself. "Right?"

"Right," Johnny answered, "by the book." It might as well be by the book, he thought. One way was as meaningless as another.

Eddie's phone rang. He listened for a moment with concern. "Alright, mom, I'll come over as soon as I can."

Eddie looked to Johnny, trying not to let the stress show. "Let's go."

"You good?" Johnny asked.

"Good," Eddie said. "She'll be okay for a little bit."

Johnny nodded, still concerned for Eddie. "What do we have on Austin Ames' will?"

"Nothing yet," Eddie answered, "but a couple of other things—the coastal commissioner that was greenlighting that development in '72 died.

"How?" Johnny asked.

"That's the strange thing. Some freak landslide up in one of the passes. The whole hillside gave way—him and his attorney were buried alive—"

"Attorney? That makes four..." Johnny said.

"Four what?" Eddie asked.

"Jessica said four deaths. The report said three deaths were attributed to the curse. What else?"

Eddie blew up. "Curse?! What curse? Dammit, Johnny, you've been holding out on me! I thought we were doing this thing together!" Eddie was genuinely hurt.

"Would you have been coming around with me if I told you this whole thing was based on an Indian curse laid down a hundred years ago?"

"Oh, jeez, my fault," Eddie said sarcastically, "I forgot to put on my hip waders when I got into this with you," Eddie scoffed.

"That's what I mean," Johnny said.

Eddie and Johnny looked at each other.

"I needed you, Eddie," Johnny said.

"For what, Johnny?" Eddie shot back without thinking, and then regretted it.

"Eddie, this one's on me. I know it's not fair to you." Johnny paused. "Your mother, is she doing okay after her fall?"

"I think," Eddie answered, unsure.

Patrick joined them at the front door. "We ready?"

Johnny looked to Eddie. "Go take care of her, Eddie. She needs you. Patrick and I can handle this. Go on."

Eddie hesitated. "Sure?" Eddie asked.

"Yeah, I'm sure," Johnny replied.

Eddie left and Johnny turned to Patrick.

"Thanks for coming down," Johnny said.

"Let's do it," Patrick said, smiling.

They entered the lobby.

Johnny nodded to the security officer as he and Patrick walked by the front desk to the elevator.

Patrick pulled out a notepad from his inner jacket pocket. "Here's what I got. Talk about a cursed family, the tanker that killed him, belonged to Sound Petroleum—a subsidiary of the Chilkat Corporation...which turns out to be working some huge Pentagon contracts. You were sure right on that one." He flipped another page. "And here's something I couldn't figure—the old man's will ordered the gardener's cottage destroyed, but it never happened."

As they arrived at the elevator, the bell rang, and the elevator door opened. No one exited.

"Don't tell me," Johnny said as they entered, "the will was made by same law firm that set up Joseph Menchaca's trust."

Johnny hit the button for the forty-eighth floor and held onto the rail with his right hand, as the elevator whirred upward.

Patrick stopped to slap his watch. "Right, how'd ya' know?" Patrick asked, slapping his watch again. "Shit. Look at this. Just bought the damn thing."

Johnny quickly checked his watch, grabbed for Patrick's wrist, turning it to read the time on his watch. The digital display read 11:22.

"No!" Johnny exclaimed.

He shot a glance up at the overhead floor indicator. It read "9". The elevator began to shake as it accelerated upward. Johnny hit the stop button. Nothing happened. He hit it again. Still nothing.

Suddenly, in a tremendous explosion, the entire floor of the elevator blew out and downward. They began falling. Johnny whipped one arm to the elbow through the railing on the elevator wall while holding a fierce grip on Patrick's wrist with his other hand. The sudden drop with the weight of their two bodies nearly pulled his arms from his sockets. Patrick was left dangling below him as they climbed higher and higher, the elevator shaft growing deeper and deeper beneath them.

Johnny strained to hold on, watching their floor approach. The elevator panel read "10, 11, 12, 13, 14, 15…" Both his hands were beginning to cramp, his strength was draining. Patrick's wrist slipped down further in his grip.

Patrick saw it and yelled, "Johnny!"

His eyes and Patrick's met. Johnny's temple bulged and his jaw clenched as he summoned his will to prevail, his fingers to hold.

The last few floors were passing. Four more to go. Time slowed. Forty…his fingers began to cramp…forty-one…he forced all his will into his finger joints…forty-two…the railing's metal edge seemed ready to cut through his fingers…forty-three…he saw the edge of that last floor dropping beneath them…one foot…two feet…three…four…

"My wife, Johnny…" Patrick gasped.

Patrick's wrist began slipping through his grip and he fell screaming into the abyss.

The elevator doors opened.

With his last bit of strength Johnny pushed himself over onto the floor, and collapsed, shuddering from the exertion, gasping for breath.

He crawled to lean over and look down into elevator shaft, listening for the impossible. There were some streaks of light from some of the floors, but the bottom, where Patrick was, was black. Just black. Not a sound.

He heard only the dull electric hum of the florescent lights and his own breathing. The elevator doors closed—-and behind them, everything was sucked down into that black hole, until some other part of him took over, pulled him back away from that empty shaft. He pushed himself onto his knees, and then stood, hitting an emergency button. The alarm sounded.

He drew his gun in a cold sweat, and marched down the corridor, toward Jessica's office. He stood to the side and pushed the door open. He drew a deep breath, and then slid through the doorway, gun first.

He walked through the darkened receptionist's office. A crack of light came through the open door into Jessica's office. He cautiously approached, afraid of what he might find. He pushed open the door. She was not at her desk.

He moved through the office, pointing the gun in sweeping arcs, toward the lavatory door. It was locked. He pulled on it hard, rattling the mechanism. Nothing. He surveyed the room again, calling through the door.

"Jessica..." he called.

No answer...he kicked the door violently—it burst open. He held his gun straight ahead, pointing into the dim light. The piped music of an old song was playing in the lavatory. The music ended—and then began, as on a loop. He saw another closed sliding door, leading to the toilet. His mind was racing, his heart pounding.

He threw open the sliding door, pointing his gun in. Empty. He returned to the sink and mirror, yanked opened the drawers. They were filled with bars of soap in four-packs. He looked up, saw himself in the mirror.

The door of the front office opened.

Johnny pressed himself against the door jam, peering out. He heard someone entering, coming into view—the cleaning woman...she took the wastepaper basket and exited. He exhaled.

Suddenly he jumped, as though touched, spinning around. A cold chill ran through him. He felt something near him, upon him, a freezing blackness crawling over him. He backed out of the bathroom, walked to the corridor.

Johnny approached the remaining elevator, looked at it.

"Damn it," he said, ducking into the stairwell for the forty-eight-floor descent.

When he got out, he walked out past the vacant guard desk onto the dimly lit marble plaza and looked up at the black monolith cutting its razor edge against the thin fog. The wind was rising and falling in gentle breezes. The moonlight illuminated the thousand panes of glass above.

Forty-eight stories of death.

The traffic was moving quietly all around him. But now the wind began to gust. He heard the sirens in the distance. This black tower with black secrets.... he would discover what lay at its foundations if he had to tear it apart slab by slab.

He craned his neck back and shouted. "What do you want?!"

He looked up at the reflections of moonlit clouds in the glass above, as though he might receive some answer. He shouted louder. "What do you want?!!!!"

"Kill me!" He shouted louder, over the rising wind. "Kill ME!!"

The wind now stormed through the plaza, between the wind tunnels of the buildings.

He shouted at the top of his lungs. "KILL ME!!!"

There was a tremendous roar and the wind rolled over him, a vast tidal wave driving him back, penetrating his mind, prying loose his footing. He fell back several steps, then fixed his footing, leaning into the wind, his eyes watering from the blasts.

Johnny watched the dark tower above. The entire building seemed to be swaying toward him, then back, and toward him again. Another gust of wind, stronger yet, blasted him, whipping and whistling its way across the plaza. The building danced and twisted as though alive.

Eddie came running up to him. "Johnny, what happened?!"

"He's dead, Eddie. Patrick's dead."

"Jesus," Eddie said. "Jesus."

"He asked for his wife. You got to go see her, Eddie. Leave someone with her, don't leave her alone." Johnny said, trying to hold it together, and started to walk away.

"Where you going, Johnny?!" Eddie asked.

"Don't leave her alone," Johnny just said.

A police officer called from the doorway of the building, "Eddie, can we get you over here?"

Eddie took hold of Johnny's arm, and nodded to him, then turned to enter the building.

Johnny looked back up at the black tower. In his mind, a voice came to him, rose above the wind, descending from the sky, or the building, or was it rising up from the ground?

The words were barely audible, but unmistakable. "I am the one you must love..." He shook with the terror as the chill ran down his spine.

The wind died down...dragging its last twisting tendrils across the now ghostly silent plaza.

'I am the one you must love...' The words resonated in Johnny's mind as they burned into his throat and hollowed out his chest.

Johnny, his head spinning, walked revolving in slow steps away from the tower, taking in the sights and sounds of the city night around him, headlights, streetlights, yellow, red, yellow green, neon signs, on and off, the office skylines, patchwork floors of lights, cars passing, cars turning, people on the street, street people drinking, horns sounding tires rolling, wind passing, people passing, voices, night voices, night songs from a corner bar, loud thoughts, quiet thoughts, killing thoughts, vengeful thoughts, thoughts of loss, family lost, lovers lost, life lost, until all those sights and sounds and thoughts swept him away in heavy waves that plunged him into the night.

He walked up the Denny regrade, his every stride stalking the pulse of the city. Anger beat in his chest, moved his legs, saw through his eyes, hunted. Hunted for its face.

He was passing the chain-link fence of a school playground. Beyond the wire, another time prevailed. He imagined the yard filled with schoolchildren. He heard their shouts and cries as they played...their laughing and crying...all things, all things he would have to see and hear, all things...

He turned left, crossed two blocks, before something drew him back down. Down the hill, into the thrumming electric groin of the city.

He crossed into the city's darker side on First Avenue. The glow and beat of neon signs selling naked girls, naked women, peep shows, dance shows, X-rated bookstores, X-rated. The lights flashed and hacked across his face, as he moved through the streets full of shamed, faceless men.

A streetwalker spied him, looked him straight in the eyes. "Hey, honey, you look like you need a blowjob." He walked on by, but his mind was talking to him...don't turn away, all right, okay, let it filter through the layers of your mind, into that ground where understanding takes hold...or dreams take hold...where spirits live...and he kept on walking.

A Mercedes cruised by, window rolling down. A black man with a fedora surveyed the territory...taking and giving...flesh, the medium of exchange in this sordid marketplace. What did they receive, those who paid the price? What did they give, those who sold the goods? Quick lust, easy lust, the price of pleasure, the seeking of pleasure...life forgotten in the cheapness of life.

Johnny cruised past dark doorways, past the homeless drunks trying to suck the last bit of happiness out of an empty wine bottle, past the swinging doors of raucous yelling angry bars, past the laughing, shouting, crying, fighting...

He passed before a collection of teenage prostitutes in miniskirts and high heels.

"Need a date, daddy?" the first called out, lifting her short skirt to the tops of her thighs.

"Lookin' for love, grandpa?" another laughed, with pearly teeth and crystalline skin.

He looked into their eyes as he passed, raking their minds, and bodies, silencing them with his own fierce reaching for sense and understanding.

Then he passed from them into the night again, into the distant beating of conga drums, pounding out the wild callings of night on the streets.

Like an animal he followed that calling. Into the night. Into release.

Because he did not know what else to follow.

He passed by a group of men warming their hands over a broken barrel with flames licking out of it, passing a bottle of wine. Born into it. Or they found their way there. A lonely corner, but warmer than his. The drumming was growing louder.

He reached an alley, the source of the drumming. He turned down it, came face to face with the conga drummer. What is it, man? What is the answer? Because I can't hold it together. Got a dream? Got a hope? I'll take what you can give me. I'm listening. Listening...

The drummer seemed not to notice him, relentlessly pounding his rhythm into the night. It's just a song, man. It's just a beat. You try to take hold of it for a riff or two. That's all you can get. Just live it, before there's no more coming down the line.

Johnny fished into his pocket, found a quarter. He tossed it into the box at the drummer's feet. He knew it was not enough. How much was enough? He reached into his back pocket and took out his wallet. Okay, take a ride with this, drummer man. He took out all the bills and tossed them down.

The drummer looked up, looked down at the wallet, nodded, looked up. He beat the drums for Johnny, and his hands spoke. So, you want the big ride? You want to cruise? Want to fly? Then fall, just fall into your dream, and when the pavement's coming up fast, just fall, fall right through it. Try to stop and you're dead. If you want to fly, you got to fall. So go...go on down the road...and the drummer beat harder into himself, into his music and into his beats, became his hands carving his own loneliness into the night.

The beat became a flood, washing Johnny out of the alley, into the darkness, into the falling rain. He wandered, one block to the next.

When he finally found his car, the rain was hitting hard, in falling sheets raking across his windshield. He hopped in, beginning to shiver from the wet, or from the witnessing. The metal and glass enclosed him in momentary comfort, encapsulating him in its self-contained world, as the rain beat his roof. A little bit of warmth when you are wet and cold, something to hold onto. Not nothing. Not nothing, Johnny.

He was going to die. So, the hell with dreams and plans, the hell with love and beauty...well, everyone's dying all the time...he began shivering violently. He had to drive.

He turned the key in the ignition, punched the heater. The engine cranked and then turned over. The rain was lightening up into a soft downpour. He pulled out into traffic. Headlights of opposing traffic danced a slow dance, the sounds of the road matching the sound of the blood beating in his temples. In his head. On the window. In his head.

He rolled down the driver window to escape its hypnotic power, keeping his eyes fixed on the road as the rain splattered the side of his face. He had been born, to drive this road, on this night, in this city. He was driving.

His mind was already there, had never left—he whipped into the circular drive of Jessica's mansion and threw open his car door. The distance to her front door seemed infinite as he crossed it, his strides reaching for a ground twisting away from him. He pushed back the waves of nausea rising in his gut, holding on to some purpose he hardly understood.

The door was ajar, as though she was expecting someone. He pushed it open. It was quiet inside. Light came down a corridor from a half-open door. He started walking.

Jessica, hearing his footsteps, opened the door to her bedroom. She was dressed in jeans and a white button-down blouse, fresh and casual.

"Johnny!" she cried out with concern when she saw his clothes soaking wet.

Johnny stopped. His heart was pounding. He did not even know why he was there. It felt good to be in her presence again. He wished it didn't.

As if in a dream, she helped him to take his coat off. "What happened, Johnny? You're so wet."

He did not answer her. Something was not right. The light in the room.

The room was lit by a dozen candles. She had said she did not like candles. It was not right, but his thoughts were not holding together, could not form. He could not tell where he began, and she ended.

He looked into her eyes, then swept her up and threw her down on the bed, his breath heaving. He kneeled over her, a predator with his prey.

Jessica was scared. "What is it, Johnny?" She spoke gently, in a caring tone, as though she believed she might say something to make it all better for him.

But he wanted to push her over the edge, into some desperate revelation.

"Eddie's partner is dead," he said. "The floor of the elevator blew out!"

"Oh my God!" She shook her head in sadness and compassion.

"Where were you?!" Johnny demanded.

Jessica suddenly seemed vulnerable, threatened, looking up at him. "You didn't get the message? To meet me here?" She was beginning to tremble. "I made something for us." Jessica nodded toward the table behind Johnny.

Johnny turned his head slowly to look over his shoulder. Behind him was a table set with linen and crystal, and a fully prepared meal, wine poured, a dark blood red wine shimmering through the cut glass... Johnny looked back at her.

"Chicken marsala–it's the only thing I ever learned to cook," she said, apologizing, her eyes opening wide like a child wrongly accused.

Johnny looked into her eyes now growing wet with tears and believed her. She really had prepared this meal. His entire world was collapsing, leaving only this single moment—and he wanted it to be true, and he wanted it to be all, so he did not have to awaken into the nightmare surrounding him on all sides.

He moved off of her to sit down on the bed beside her. Stress was cutting through his belly like a knife, slicing him in half—

But she put her hand over his. It was warm. The choice was easy.

Jessica looked upon him with compassion. She saw the cut on his cheek. "It got you, too.... I'm so sorry..."

"What...?" he asked, without understanding anything.

She laid her hand to the side of his face, gently caressing his cheek. He let his hand ride down over the top of hers. She reached out, wrapping an arm around him, and with her other hand, began undoing the top two buttons of her blouse. She gently pulled his face toward her chest, holding his head tight against her breasts.

Slowly, he began kissing up the hollow of her throat, up round her chin, to her lips–their eyes met. Gently he drew her lips to his, closing the two worlds between them—suddenly, she turned her cheek away, frightened.

He gently took her cheeks between his hands, turning her face back toward his, bringing her lips back to his. Again, she turned, again he brought her lips back...and kissed her...she began to tremble. She was almost shaking as she placed her palms against the top of his chest, pushing him away, at first softly, as he held her near, and then harder. Still, he would not release her.

He did not know in that moment what drove him to oppose his will to hers. Only he had glimpsed an unknown face through a doorway, and he would fight with his life to hold on to it. He kissed her until tears filled her eyes, ran down her cheeks... until finally, uncertain, she began responding...haltingly matching his movements... with growing passion discovering his dream because it was her dream.... words came to her lips, as words she had never said before, to any man... words barely audible. "I want you."

Her words found him, alone, unprotected. She knew. Emboldened, too, by the walls crashing down within her, she said louder, in a new voice, "I want you... I want you, Johnny... I want you..."

He received her, kept receiving her until all other voices within him were defeated. With one hand he ripped down the buttons of her blouse, taking her breast in his mouth, reaching to unbuckle his belt. She pushed her jeans down to her thighs, naked underneath, growing wilder as she released herself to her own passions. She turned around underneath him, pushing her backside up in the air toward him.

"Where do you want me, where do you want me?" she pleaded for an answer.

For Johnny, a ripple passed across the face of the dream, became a wave, like sounds disturbing the sleeper's world. He struggled to hold onto his dream, dragging her with him even as she was waking from it.

He took control. Gently, he turned her back over, began kissing her neck, and up to her lips.

"No... no... no." Jessica began crying again, turning her lips away, moving his head into the hollow of her neck, stroking his hair.

"Johnny..." It was an unfinished sentence, calling him toward her, asking him to stop. "Johnny," she said, more firmly.

Already he was moving his pelvis against her, now purely sexual, animal, now without lust, without even desire, but with some unknown purpose that he knew risked destroying them both. But where was he taking her? Where would she take him?

"No, no, don't..." She protested, moving underneath him. "Love me, love me," she pleaded, then gasped as he penetrated her.

"...Johnny...ah...ah...no-no no-" no-no-no-..." She pulled him deeply into her, began moving her hips—then froze. Began moving again. Stopped again. She was crying. But growing more excited, breathing in short gasps, sobbing, "I wanted you, I wanted you, Johnny," as though it could not be, as though that hope was already lost, even as she joined him in a greater and greater rhythm of passion...until..." No, no, you're going to make me—you're going to make me—no, no, no, no."

As she grew more excited, she began panting a phrase. "I, I, I am the one, I am the one, ahhhh, I am, I am..."

He reached into her eyes, released his mind to her, released his dream to hers,

dreamed with her...

...a dark figure, holding up a torch, holding the hand of a barefoot

seven-year-old-girl dressed in a nightgown, leading her through a dimly lit underground tunnel with a floor of dirt...terror in her eyes.

"...the one you must, you must, you must love..." she said the words softly, but they screamed from her soul in an anguished torrent.

He followed her, into her pain, into...

...a candle-lit cottage...where a young girl lay naked on a bed, an old man above her, with mad red eyes. He began copulating with her. And things swooping down, flying, approaching, images arising and vanishing, passing before here and over her, one, and then another...

...snarling jaws of wolves...glaring red eyes...snarling jaws attacking, claws leaping...

... the images of wolves with burning red eyes became the faces of her older brothers, David, William, Mark, as children, leering down at her from an overhead balcony encircling a large parlor, as they sat, legs dangling, watching Jessica as a seven-year-old girl being led away, hand in hand, by her stepfather—and the helplessness in Jessica's eyes, the wordless, unanswered appeal to her brothers for help as she looked up to their faces...

But he could not hold there. He found himself thrown back into the moment, to see her face, crying, distant, as she remembered, terrified by demons, silently screaming for the kind of love she could never know.

"I am the one—I am the one, don't, don't...don't, don't," she panted...

He tried to calm her, soothe her, but he did not know what to say. He stroked her cheeks...but then he saw, in her glassy terrified eyes, the words were not coming from her, but at her—they were not her words.

Jessica broke down into bitter crying, possessed, controlled... "I can't, I can't love you, Johnny."

Johnny hardly heard her. He was stroking her hair, breathing in her suffering, traveling to another time and place to be near her. For an instant, he believed he had found her, was really touching her.

"Jessica..." he invoked her name...

And for a second, she came to him, opening fully that doorway into herself, filling his blood and senses with the warm currents of a momentary heaven. And then, in that brief instant of joining him, she cried for help. "Johnny!" She cried out.

Then her eyes went blank. "Get off." She squirmed underneath him. "Get off of me!" she screamed, pushing him off of her.

The force of her words hurled Johnny from her world back into a world no longer his own, an empty world made suspect by the very journey from which he had just returned. He pushed himself up onto his hands and knees above her.

She pushed him the rest of the way off.

Then she turned over on her belly, again raising herself on her knees, her head down against the bed.

"Where do you want me? Where do you want me?" she said as before, but now with an air of desperate, uncontrollable self-loathing.

Johnny wanted to turn his eyes but was unable. Instead, he did the only thing he could think of. He gently turned her back over, and softly repeated her own words back to her. "Jessica, 'I am the one you must love'..."

Jessica smiled, uncomprehending.

Johnny persisted, softly but firmly. "Jessica, 'I am the one you must love'..."

Jessica shook her head, back and forth, again.

Johnny spoke more harshly, with authority, "'I am the one you must love'."

What finally triggered her, he did not know. She answered, in a ghost-like voice, as though echoing a nursery rhyme from the past. "I am the one you must love, to save you from the killer's above." Tears flooded into her eyes, and then a wild, uncontrollable fear.

Johnny drew back. "Who are the killer's above, Jessica?"

Jessica just looked at him, then spoke as if from a distant place.

"You look so strong in the candlelight."

Johnny tried to hold her gaze, but her attention seemed to be wandering. "Jessica, who are the killers above?"

She said dreamily, "This ceiling looks familiar."

Johnny shook her. "Jessica!"

She continued as though she did not hear him. "That's what I remember most...there were spots on it...sometimes it was like all those spots were dancing..."

"Who are the killers above?" he drilled her.

She began humming, a sweet and loving children's lullaby, Hm-hm, hmm-himm-hm...

Suddenly she became immediately and fully present.

"Don't you know, Johnny...people who have died..."

"What people?" Johnny asked desperately.

"People who have died that you should have loved. They watch you from above and take you away with them if you stop giving your love."

"Give your love to who? Who told you this?" Johnny, stunned, asked, then noticed that Jessica was staring over his shoulder at something on the wall.

Johnny looked where she was looking—it was a mounted wolf's head.

Jessica was speaking... "Candles aren't so bad...when you're not alone," she said. Then, mechanically, she got up and threw on her pants, grabbing her ripped blouse.

He watched as she walked into the bathroom.

Johnny threw on his pants as she closed the door and locked it behind herself with a loud metallic click.

Johnny heard her turn the faucet. The sound of running water poured into the strange silence beginning to fill the room.

Johnny strode to the door, knocked. "Jessica." No answer. He glanced toward the mounted wolf's head, then walked over to it. Its eyes were a dull red, but strangely, when he moved below it, almost glowing.

He took one of the candles and waved the flame over the face, illuminating it, then slowly moved it under and around the chin. A sound came from the bathroom. He glanced in that direction, still holding the candle under the wolf's head. When he looked back, the eyes were gleaming red.

He spun toward the bathroom door. "Jessica!" He raced back to the door, knocked on it hard. "Jessica!!!" Still no answer. He rattled the doorknob. "Jessica!!!"

Johnny heaved his shoulder against the door, breaking it open. It was dark inside. He grabbed a candle and entered. It was a two-room bathroom—she was not in the front. Water was running in the large sunken tub in the back room. He turned a corner, stepped down to the curtained tub, drew back the curtain—she was gone.

He was in octagonal room with mirrors for walls. He looked all around, examining the floor, the mirrored ceiling, the walls, seeing nothing. He pulled out his gun, fired down into a mirror. It shattered, but as if in slow motion. He saw the trajectory of every fragment, like the glass on the plaza of David's death, like the windows of Mark's apartment, now bursting into a glimmering mocking revelation—but behind the broken mirror, only a bare wall remained.

He fired again into another mirror, and then another, and another, and another. Until one mirror shattered, and he found himself looking down a dimly lit corridor, partially illuminated by a few dust-covered red lightbulbs wired into hanging two-plug metal outlet boxes strung on more wires running along the walls of the tunnel near the ceiling.

He entered, advancing cautiously. Above him, red eyes glowed in the darkness. He stopped, then moved the candle closer. The eyes seemed to burn brighter. It was another larger wolf's head, jaws gaping open with huge sharp teeth.

He continued, more heads–more glowing red eyes——four more mounted heads, staggered along the corridor walls every ten feet on either side. He began racing down the tunnel. It led to another door—locked. He kicked it open. Flames exploded through the doorway, driving him back into the tunnel. He looked back to see a wall of flame was rushing toward him.

He charged forward through the flames of the doorway, and emerged into the gardener's cottage, empty except for an old twin poster bed with an ancient bare gray mattress, and closed black drapes, now all aflame. Coughing and gasping in the smoke, he managed to yell, "Jessica!!!"

He looked desperately for the door, rushed outside—the night had exploded into pounding sheets of rain, and thundering bolts of lightning.

He ran through a corridor of shrubs—just in time to see a black limousine disappearing down the driveway. He heard glass shattering and exploding, looking back to see flames shooting through Jessica's bedroom window.

He raced to his car, jumped in, whipped it around to pursue her. He began losing ground, his view obscured by a broken wiper blade. He followed her through several lights, up and down two hills.

Suddenly the limousine's tires squealed, and it accelerated at full throttle, whipping around a corner. Johnny floored his gas pedal, chasing her at breakneck speed. In the distance, he saw the limousine turn another corner.

When he turned after it, the limousine had vanished. But he had no doubt where he would find her. He did a U-turn and raced toward the Chilkat Tower Plaza.

He found the limousine parked all the way up on the plaza, immediately in front of the Chilkat Corporation skyscraper. He pulled up thirty feet back, jumped out, and approached the limousine. As he drew nearer, he saw Phillip's head leaning against the fractured stained red glass of the driver side window.

He opened the door, and the Phillip's body fell half out. There was a red bullet hole in his right temple.

He raced into the Chilkat Tower, into the elevator. Whipping off his belt, he threaded and buckled it through the elevator railing, and grabbed hold, winding it several times around his wrist. He knew where she was going.

He hit the button for the seventeenth floor, looked to the overhead display panel, and began counting the floors, finally reaching the fourteenth, fifteenth, sixteenth... he reached the seventeenth. The doors opened.

Johnny leapt out of the elevator. He strode down the corridor, turned onto the open floor. He saw Jessica sitting, barefoot, knees tucked up under her chin, inside the frame of the blown-out window. Her shoes and the yellow police ribbon torn from the window lay in a bundle near her feet.

She was holding her hand in front of her face, palm outward. High winds were blowing and whistling, flapping her clothes. Johnny approached to within a few feet and stopped. He could see the city lights beyond through the open window frame.

She spoke to him softly, looking at her hand. "When I was child, I used to imagine that I could see right through my hand..."

Johnny slipped closer. "What could you see through your hand?"

"Whatever was there. It was all there—I just never knew if I was."

Johnny listened for a moment to see if she would continue. He could see the tears in her eyes. He asked, "And now?"

"...I just want to go home," she said.

"I want to take you home, Jessica." Johnny stepped closer, reached out to touch her.

"You can't, Johnny..." She whipped around with a revolver in her hand to point it into his face. "...but we can go together."

Johnny froze.

Jessica shook her head in disbelief, amused. "Did it ever occur to you, Johnny, that I really just want to be left alone..."

Johnny slowly, cautiously, took one step back. She did not seem to notice.

She laughed as she cocked the trigger.

"Jessica..." Johnny spoke soothingly...

"...it's okay, Johnny, it's just a nightmare..." she whispered, still holding the gun toward his face. "Who dies—when—does it really matter? Eventually, I'll be alone—you, too...you, too, Johnny." She smiled softly, waving the gun. "Get back!"

Johnny inched back two more steps, staying within arm's reach of her gun.

"...only, if I go first now, I won't be able to watch anyone else go." Jessica fired over his left shoulder. "Listen to me!" Then she said very softly, "Are you listening? I want you to listen..."

She continued, patiently and gently explaining her purposes. "You said you could love me...now I have to see where I am going... see it perfectly," she explained, softly rubbing her temple with the muzzle of the gun. "So, you will go first?"

Johnny watched her every move, saying nothing.

She snaked the aim of the gun down toward his crotch. "I have enjoyed loving you...will you take off your shirt for me, Johnny?"

Johnny shook his head, 'no.'

"You will. Do you know why a man rapes a woman? They never come you know. He can't admit the power of life and death she holds over him. Power is either of this world or the next, and the next is a bet that may never pay off, isn't it?"

Johnny surveyed the room, looking for cover.

"Oh, it's nothing personal, Johnny, if I could ever have loved a man, it would have been you." Jessica fired over his right shoulder.

She waved the gun toward his waist. "Undo your belt."

Johnny stared straight ahead, shaking his head in refusal.

Jessica regarded his protest with a slight smile, then lifted the gun back toward his head. "Where do you want it?"

Johnny, in a calm, almost transcendental state, now looked directly into her eyes. "I love you, Jessica."

She fixed the gun sight on his heart. "And I'm sure you do," she agreed. "My stepfather loved me, too. 'I love you, my little one,' he would say, 'now love me because I am the one you must love, to save you from the killers above.' Just a pretty rhyme, don't you think? ...I only remember the pain."

Jessica stiffened her arms to aim, then closed her eyes.

Johnny felt no fear. Strangely, he felt a sense of light all around him. He knew he would be joining her, released from all the pain burning inside him.

Was that all there was to this moment before death? All those loose ends...but life would go on without him, and those loose ends would not really be that important to anyone...he believed she was going to pull the trigger.

But she did not. She dropped her arms, opening her eyes, shaking her head.

Johnny exhaled his suspended breath.

"No, he'd still be there..." She leaned back, again casually rubbing the muzzle of the revolver against her temple. "Do you know what I mean?"

He shook his head, but he knew.

She sighed, "I'm so tired, Johnny...."

It was more than an earthly exhaustion he saw overtaking her.

She stepped out of the window frame, walking a few steps to one side to sit down on a stacked pile of sheet-rock.

She continued, "You knew I wasn't going to kill you, didn't you? Oh, I don't care that all that you really wanted was to fuck me." The words rolled off her tongue, hard, angry. "The rest of the time it was really nice, Johnny...and really, it was me that was being unfaithful..."

Suddenly, the silhouette of a human form rose up from behind Jessica—

Johnny whipped out his gun, aiming it at her, shouting.

"NOOOO!!!!!"

—a shotgun blast exploded—Johnny was struck in the chest, thrown back five feet, landing flat on his back.

Joseph Menchaca, enraged and red-eyed, no longer blind, stood behind Jessica, holding a double-barrel sawed-off shotgun. His hand reached from behind to caress her bare throat with a red carnation, over her breastbone, up over her chin, the flower petals and then his fingers caressing her lips, to finally caress her hair back away from her forehead.

Jessica, feeling the familiar touch, gasped, in a strange mixture of terror and security. "Tears flooded from her eyes. "You came back..."

Joseph placed his throat to the crown of her head, so that his head rested over and above hers, and then placed the barrel of the shotgun under her chin. He began sweetly, lovingly humming a child's lullaby. Hm-hm, himm-hmmm-hm...

He moved his other hand down her throat to her breast, caressing it, freeing it from her shirt.

Jessica looked toward Johnny's fallen figure as Joseph ran his fingers through

her hair. "He'll never hurt you, my little one...Hm-hm, himm-hmmm-hm..." His hand pulled back the dual triggers of the shotgun.

"You were the only one who loved me." For a moment only his breathing could be heard, until he whispered, "Your father stole your mother from me....and now you, you, too have been unfaithful to me...."

His thumb began to push against the dual triggers.

A shot rang out. The bullet exploded red through his forehead. His head snapped backward and then forward, his eyes focusing on Johnny with deadly hate and rage. Like a re-animated corpse, Joseph lifted the shotgun, aiming it toward Johnny's chest... and then dropped dead onto his back behind her.

Ten feet away, Johnny was kneeling on one knee, holding his pistol in two hands, locked in deadly concentration. The shotgun blast had ripped his shirt apart, revealing the skull and-crossbones armor vest underneath.

Jessica was looking at him in horror, anguish, terror, a hundred mixed emotions, her gaze tearing deeper into him with every breath.

Then she stood and turned, to look back down at the body. She leaned down and picked up the red carnation, and with the other hand slowly reaching toward Joseph with an outstretched hand, fingers trembling.

Johnny watched, entranced.

She lowered herself to her knees beside him, placing the carnation on his chest. Then she moved her fingers toward his lips. She barely touched his lips with her fingers, letting them trail off his chin as she leaned closer to him...and closer...

Then she stopped, and slowly drew back, to kneel upright, turning her eyes toward Johnny. And for the first time, for that brief moment, Johnny saw her, all that she was, all that she would ever be.

Johnny was standing now, holding the gun down by his side.

Jessica leaned over and picked up the shotgun, letting it hang down by her side. He watched as she shifted her grip, moving the barrel into her left hand, clasping the stock with her right hand, her finger on the trigger.

Johnny aimed at her chest.

She did not move. The shotgun was pointed toward the floor,

He could hear her breathing.

An eternity passed, seconds becoming moments. She began raising the shotgun toward him. Now there was nothing left. In matching time, Johnny began ever so lightly squeezing the trigger, aiming at her chest.

The shotgun now pointed toward him at waist-level, off to his right side. If she swung the aim toward him, he would fire one shot into her heart.

He waited.

Suddenly, she dropped the gun. Tears began pouring from her eyes.

Johnny lowered his gun and put a hand out toward her.

She stepped back. He took another step toward her. She began taking slow steps backward, moving toward the open window.

Across the distance, he reached toward her with an outstretched hand.

But with each step she moved another mile away, another continent away, until the heels of her feet hung over the edge.

"Don't do it, Jessica," he said, knowing his words would mean nothing.

She neither heard him, nor moved. Her mind was drifting, tears were running down her cheeks.

"You don't have to, Jessica."

The sound of running footsteps and voices drew nearer.

"Johnny!" It was Eddie, running toward them with another policeman.

They saw the dead body, and Jessica standing in the empty window frame.

Johnny held up his hand, and they froze.

Jessica was seeing no one.

No one moved or spoke.

He surveyed the distance between himself and Jessica, too far to make a lunge. He watched her, prepared to try.

Jessica began slowly raising her arms, and began to sway, first forward and then back. She closed her eyes. She was going to do it. He knew she was going to do it.

As she swayed forward again, he leaped. She began swaying back. With his second bound, he saw her balance moving over the edge—with his third, she released herself, but he had reached her now, throwing his arm around her waist, sweeping her from the edge.

She was pliant, moving with him, as though expecting no other end than to be back in his arms.

She was glad to be near him again, as a child enjoying the moment, not caring what lay ahead.

Two policemen took hold of her by her arms on either side, and he released her.

"Have you been to Paris in the spring, Johnny? I have a pied-a-terre in the 7th," she said lightly. "We can drink wine on the balcony and watch the lights go on at night on the Eiffel tower."

Now a police officer was saying something to Eddie. Eddie was asking something of him, but their mouths were moving without words, without sound...

Johnny looked into her eyes for a last time. The city lights through the open window had turned her blue eyes violet.

She met his gaze, with a look that told him she understood everything completely, everything except that shadow that she had never been without. "Come see me, Johnny..." she said.

Johnny nodded, not knowing what he was nodding about, as the police officers walked her away.

Eddie looked down at the body. "Joseph Menchaca?"

"Raymond Ames. Or his ghost," Johnny said, looking down at the body. "The curse took his mind and soul long ago."

"Her stepfather was the curse?" Eddie asked.

"He became it," Johnny answered. "Austin must have used him to get what he wanted from Mary Ames, then cut him out of everything—the land, the corporation, the family," Johnny answered. "Until he got it all back. Even their daughter..."

"Her, Jesus..." Eddie just said.

"He killed them all. I'm sure. Mary Ames, Joseph Menchaca, Austin, David, Mark," Johnny said. "Not William. Not William," Johnny mused.

"Killed for what? The land? The money? For what?" Eddie asked.

"In the end, for the only thing that mattered to him...for her, Eddie," Johnny answered, "for her..."

"Jesus...Jesus..." Eddie said. "You're lucky you made it out alive."

"Did I?" Johnny offered, as he looked back up to see Jessica being taken away.

"Come on," Eddie said, putting his arm around Johnny's shoulder.

Johnny and Eddie began walking out together.

Eddie, shaking his head in sympathy, added, "Love's a many splendored thing...I got your back, partner, always have, always will."

Not Far from Paris

Two weeks later, Johnny traveled to the Bellingham State Mental Hospital. He had not expected to be returning to such a place.

He found himself questioning the doctor. "Raymond Ames killed Austin Ames and then Joseph Menchaca, but then he came here...I mean, with all his money, why didn't he just leave the country?"

"Hard to say...maybe at first he really thought he could get some help, or maybe he just didn't want to be far from Jessica. Maybe as he got worse, when Jessica left to live her life in Europe, he realized this was the perfect place to hide his real psychosis."

"Hiding his insanity in a mental institute—that's something" Johnny admitted.

"Tragic, for everyone he hurt, like some force more powerful than his own personal psychology took hold of Joseph—I mean Raymond—but what rage makes a man destroy his own daughter—stepdaughter—then seek vengeance against his boys for witnessing his own depravity..."

"The curse..." Johnny said. "It possessed him."

"A curse?" the doctor asked.

Johnny spoke half to himself. "...the dead are not powerless..."

"What's that?" the doctor asked.

Johnny shook his head, changing the subject. "How is Jessica doing?"

"This way. You can see for yourself." The doctor beckoned for Johnny to join him as he walked down a corridor. "Victims of traumatic psychosis like this, it's hard to say whether they really heal, or ever can. They can only hope to just become functional again, try to keep the world around them within boundaries they can cope with."

They turned the corner and stopped, viewing Jessica from a few yards away. Sitting on an outdoor sofa under a canopy, she was happily engaged in an animated discussion with the patient next to her.

The doctor observed her for a moment. "She will always offer that impossible and contradictory love of a child. I would guess that her emotional growth was arrested when the molestation began at seven—what might have lay ahead for her...her whole childhood, who she might have become as a woman..." He shook his head. "...was stolen forever."

Johnny watched Jessica, his love for her and his own pain rising up within him.

The doctor saw it and said, "In many ways, she is a remarkable soul. I'm sorry, Mr. Hammond."

Johnny kept staring. The doctor touched his shoulder and left, leaving Johnny alone again on the border of two worlds.

When he approached her, she looked up and smiled. She was breezy, carefree, delighted to see him.

"Hi, Johnny!"

Just like that. Like nothing had happened.

"Hello, Jessica. Can I sit down with you?" he asked.

Jessica patted the sofa.

Johnny sat down beside her, keeping an easy tone, "So how are you doing?"

Jessica, upbeat, kicked in, "I'll tell you. The administration here is living in the dark ages. I haven't seen the rack yet, but I'm sure they're hiding one in some basement somewhere..."

Johnny could not help but smile. "Doc says you're making some progress." Had the doctor said that?

Jessica smirked, tossing off, "How kind of him, but he couldn't find his own ass with a flashlight, excuse my

French. I observed some disassociated behavior in him when he was testing me..."

Johnny just looked at her.

She touched his leg and whispered, "I know you wanted me here until some of the problems blow over." She nodded happily with their conspiracy, continuing, "You know, it's terrible what happened to my brothers. But brothers should take care of their little sisters..."

A sudden chill ran down Johnny's spine. She turned fully toward him, her heart opening, and her face lighting up like a woman in love.

"Just get me a hearing, and I'll take it from there. There's nothing to worry about. You can come back to Paris with me."

Johnny listened to her with sadness, and compassion.

She continued. "I have a home there. We can drink wine on the Champs-Elysee." She smiled, her eyes growing ever warmer.

Her blue eyes changed to a brighter blue in the sunlight. Johnny had never noticed.

He wanted to give her something. "They say there is going to be a once-in-a- century meteor shower on Sunday." He pointed into the low sky. "To the south."

She smiled, seeing through to his charity.

"This doesn't have to haunt us for the rest of our lives, you know, Johnny," she said.

She took his hand gently on her cheek, and she nuzzled her face into his palm.

"Take care of yourself, Jessica, will you" Johnny said, and then gently slipped his hand from hers.

She looked up at him, concerned. "You too, Johnny."

Johnny stood and began to leave.

She added, "Don't leave your dreams behind...they don't have to be all bad..." She gave a little smile.

Johnny smiled back, touched by her words. He knew he would not see her again.

For One Image

Johnny entered his loft, dropping his keys onto the counter.

The last rays of sunlight from the low afternoon sun were pouring through his windows. He reached down to a coffee table to switch on a lamp. At the lamp's base was his Hasselblad camera. He stared at it, not remembering having left it there. He was sure he had taken no other photograph from it since the one he had taken of David. He took it into his darkroom, removed the film.

Under the soft red light, he used the tongs to work the photographic image, under the developers' chemicals. The doorbell rang. Without thinking, Johnny hit the door buzzer, and someone entered.

"Johnny?" someone called out. "You there, buddy?" It was Eddie. He continued working the photograph, gently, expertly, agitating the chemical bath. "Got you some Chinese," Eddie shouted. "Man, freezin' out there."

He heard Eddie approaching the darkroom door.

Johnny called to him through the door. "Hey, turn off the lights, and come on in."

Eddie entered speaking and Johnny listened, while looking down to the photograph immersed in the developing solution, watching as the shape of a face began emerging...

...slowing appearing under the clear liquid...

"Lab guys been working overtime. The explosive trace we found on the old man's hands. Once they knew what to look for, they were able to identify minute particles to match up with the elevator and seventeenth floor explosions."

Johnny nodded and Eddie continued, "The old man must have rigged the bomb pack on the woman, too. What he was using was quiet, powerful, completely clean—real hot stuff, army-classified top secret."

"The crane?" Johnny asked, seeing emerging through the clear development fluid

...mesmerizing eyes...

"The control box had been set up to accept a remote signal...must've been some kind of weapons genius," Eddie said.

He already knew when he asked. "...and the window that killed David'?"

...full lips...

"Nothing—still looking like a freak accident. Maybe the wind. Same with the power lines.

"Not an accident..." Johnny intoned.

"We found the gun that killed the chauffeur on him...but the killing on the train, Johnny..." Eddie hesitated..." all we know for sure is that Raymond Ames couldn't have been on that train when it happened."

...an angelic face...

"Will Jessica Ames be charged?"

...promising peace and spiritual grace...

"Does it matter? She's never getting out of Bellingham," Eddie said.

"Besides, Patrick was the only one who thought he saw her get on that train—unless you testify that you saw her."

...joyful...

"I didn't see her," Johnny said.

...radiant...

"Johnny?" Eddie asked again.

"I didn't see her, Eddie." Johnny confirmed.

...childlike...

"The board voted the land back into trust?" Johnny asked, entranced with the face he saw emerging in the photograph.

Eddie nodded. "Unanimously...for the sole and perpetual use of the tribe..."

"Then it's over," Johnny said.

"You want me to post a car downstairs for a couple of days?" Eddie asked. "Or I could stay with you for a couple of days."

"Too romantic, Eddie," Johnny joked, "No, I'll be okay," Johnny said, looking to Eddie while putting his tongs into the developing tray.

"I'm picking you up for lunch tomorrow. Get some sleep, huh?" Eddie pounded Johnny lightly on his chest and made his way out.

Johnny looked back down at the photograph. For a long moment, he did not move. He waited as the ripples in the clear developing solution passed, resolving into a perfect window revealing the face below.

He was not surprised. It did not matter how her image had appeared on that negative. He knew from this time forward, whenever his shutter opened on an empty room, or a dark room, or a room with too much light, he would find her face on his negative. Jessica.

In the odd glance or gesture, or the sudden gust of wind, he would always feel her presence haunting the distance between himself and others, throwing open doorways in the random moments of his life.

Maybe love, but never their love. Never that love.

But for her, he knew it had really been over before it had begun. She did not have to jump through that empty window. Someone had pushed her through a long time ago. And that part of her that had fallen, that lived so far away inside her, would always rule her. She would always be at that crossroads where a terrified child stood alone and was forced to choose one world over another just to survive another day.

He put the photograph down on the table.

He walked out of his darkroom into his studio and stood before his windows. He glanced over to the wall with Lara's portraits. He looked out through his windows across the Puget Sound, to the west. Upon the distant peaks of the Olympic Mountains, the high snow was still moonlit like a shining silver crest.

On his table was the photograph of David Ames, standing framed before the window against those same peaks. He stared down at it, then back to those jagged snow-capped peaks across the waters.

He opened one of the windows, felt the chilling wind rush in over his face.

He let it enter him. He let the cold pour through his throat and skin into his veins, until he could feel the heat of his heart warring against it.

The world began to breathe again. The wind was in his lungs, and he could feel the floor beneath his feet.

There was another voice now, too, unadmitted for so many years.

He could feel her near now, as he opened to his memories of the overflowing richness and warmth of their times together. Lara. He had loved her as he would never love a woman again.

 Or would he?

Somewhere, between love and friendship, between the one and the few, he would have to find a new horizon.

Only one thought came to him. He held on to it. Where there were shadows, there had also to be light.